My Memory Told Me a Secret

JEREMY C BRADLEY-SILVERIO DONATO

Eiffel Tower Press
Paris | London | New York
www.eiffeltowerpress.com
@jeremycbradley

Cover photography: ©Fran Mart / Adobe Stock

My Memory Told Me a Secret / Bradley-Silverio Donato. — 1st ed.
ISBN 978-1-7332603-0-5

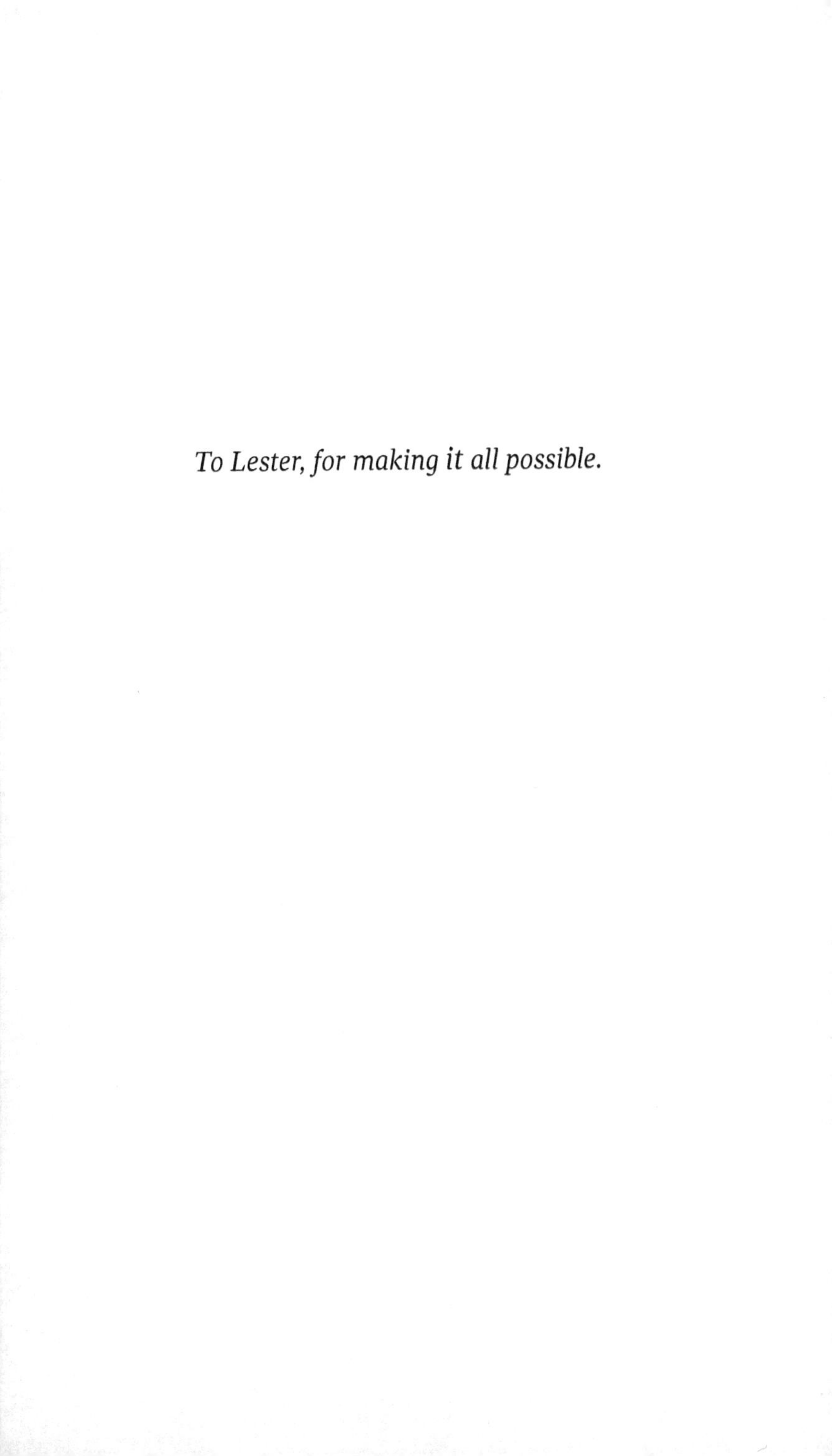

To Lester, for making it all possible.

ONE

Time sweats in the middle of the night when all the other dimensions are sleeping.

— JOY LADIN

London smelled of nothing, which is to say it smelled of everything melded together into an indistinguishable aroma. It was mid-Autumn and, on the tube, a man with soft features gazed at the advertisement boards hanging above the heads of the passengers sat opposite.

THIS IS THE END OF DATING. WE'RE SERIOUS.

Yea right, thought Austin, reading the sign plastered over a particularly dire-looking set of nine-to-fivers. When did dating apps start marketing on the underground?

He opened his bag and pulled out a notebook. Keeping a diary was an on-again, off-again habit developed over years of on-again, off-again thera-py. Like years of counselling, journaling became both a comfort and distraction. The oilcloth book had the familiarity of an old lover of the sort you meet for sex and cognac but with whom you nev-er get too attached.

He began a nervous flicking of the pages. It was a catch-all of meeting minutes, reminders, diary entries, and doodles. Not quite professional, not quite personal. And there a quarter of the way through between a grocery shopping list and notes on a client brief, was the entry he had been looking for. Fourteen names, fourteen dates which had all gone nowhere. That wasn't fair, really. A few progressed to a second date and one or two others progressed to the bedroom. None had been the end of dating.

As passengers shuffled in droves on and off the train car, Austin did a mental rifle-through of the dating profile of the man he matched with: late twenties, muscly, works in the public sector, likes include Italian food and hip-hop music. As a thir-ty-four-year-old, ectomorphic criminal barrister, this new potential was exotic, a break from Austin's everyday routine. He got a little giddy as he reached for his iPhone to shuffle through smil-ing selfies and posed portraits. But what am I do-ing? he thought. He had let himself be taken in by low-quality photos of what could/might/potentially be a somewhat/possibly handsome fellow. He didn't operate on certainties these days. Realising this about himself was scary. Very nearly making up his mind to alight at the next station and ride the train going in the opposite direction, he heard the announcement: *Next stop: London Bridge.* Too late then. This was his stop.

Some guys set out to make their mark on the world by being truly good at something. These are the guys that will things into existence. A better job? Work a year or two in a crappy position at a big-name place; doors will open. A gorgeous girlfriend? Date a string of not-so-hot women to make the others jealous. These are men of action. Then there are guys like Noah Hakim. Shit mostly happened *to* Noah. That was how he saw it, anyway. And those were the thoughts swirling around his head as he stepped into the pub opposite London Bridge station forty-five minutes before his date.

Noah never matched with anyone even remotely attractive on dating apps. He swiped right on easy boys, girls out for a fun night, people of both sexes that never wrote back after the first hello. It had all gotten old. As such, it was all too familiar terrain when he got a quick 'Hello there' from a man called Austin a few days back. Sure, Austin didn't appear to be the average Tinder variety of gay — in most of his pics he wore a suit or polo shirt, the hairs on his head never out of place — in sum, he looked uptight. But Noah was smarter than this. He knew how easy it was to FaceTune a photo, to stage success, hell even to invent interesting facts about yourself. He kept his own profile a simple mix of unedited photos shot on his old two megapixel camera mixed in with one or two identification card-style images he mopped from a mate down in the HR department of the Midwifery Council where he worked. Still, seventy-two hours went gone by and Austin was still responding to all Noah's messages. That was something.

'What can I get you?' asked the bartender.

'Pabst Blue Ribbon and a shot of tequila,' said Noah taking one of the barstools.

'At the same time?' asked the bartender, confused. Right away he sensed his present customer was distracted. A guy like that, you ask him what he wants, he should ask for a good English pint. Not a PBR, not a shot of tequila, and definitely not back-to-back. Bartenders are keen observers of human nature.

Noah grunted. The bartender went about getting the drinks. Returning, he could see his customer mumbling words to himself, almost as though a conversation was being rehearsed.

'Do you wanna talk about it, mate?' He said this carefully. The bartender did not want to come off as some kind of South London creepy Lloyd from The Shining.

There was silence for a few moments. The bartender began wiping down the countertop.

'It never gets any easier,' Noah said finally.

'Tell me about it,' the bartender said, not as a question. He understood Noah's struggle. In his position, he felt he could understand anyone's struggle.

'I've got a date, round the corner in half an hour or so.' Noah took a final gulp from the beer bottle and slid it across the counter. 'Hit me with another, will ya?'

'What's she like?' said the bartender, putting down the bottle.

Noah smirked, considering his options. Why bother with details? Surely the important thing was to get sufficiently buzzed before meeting Austin.

'She's great, yea, I mean really beautiful like.' Noah threw back the shot of tequila and reached for the PBR.

'Sounds like you got nothing to worry 'bout then, mate.' The pub began to fill up, as bars tend to do around that time of the afternoon, and the bartender needed to see to his other clientele.

'Yea, right,' said Noah. 'That's right.'

He swallowed the remainder of his second beer and stood up. He noticed that the bartender was rather attractive with his scruffy facial hair and ball cap on backwards.

'How do I look?' he said, putting out his arms and doing a little spin that seemed to the bartender to be awfully camp.

'Smashing, mate. I'm sure you'll wow her.' He said this last bit rather more loudly to emphasise the point to any of the other customers listening on.

Noah sat back down again. 'But I want to look *fabulous* ...'

He was getting loud now, and the bartender put down a large glass of tap water in front of him.

'... like don't-you-want-to-fuck-me or how about run-off-with-me-somewhere. That kind of hot.'

The bartender winced. 'Drink the water, man. You need to get it together.'

Austin propped up against a concrete pillar outside the café. Bad quality profile pictures were all he had to go on, and he was sure to miss Noah Hakim if he waited indoors. But as Noah approached him with a warm hello, Austin realised it would have taken an icicle's chance in a forest fire to miss someone like him. Noah's eyes swirled like liquid gold with hues of amber and green, never quite settling in one place. The redbone tint of his skin, the thinness of his physique, and the closely cropped hair on his head and face all called out to Austin in some primal, subconscious way, Austin being the exact opposite in both looks and confidence. Both men dressed in denim. Both wore black hats. But where Noah came off prepossessing — skinny jeans, fitted cap — Austin appeared the Northwest London chap he very much was — boot-cut slimline jeans and one of those little caps that sits on the top of the head, very French in its felt fabric construction.

Noah ordered a double mocha, something that before today Austin didn't know existed, his own choice generally limited to a filter coffee or, if he felt posh, a cappuccino.

'So how do you define yourself?' Noah said, swerving a little as he sat down.

Never much for the sort of open-ended question that can lead down rabbit holes, Austin shot

Noah a double take. 'In relation to what,' he said, 'my work, my personal life, ...?'

'In relation to yourself.' An unheard *obviously* was attached to this.

Austin paused for several seconds, stumbling over thoughts morphing into words. 'Hey, let's discuss our jobs? Or something easier to settle into?'

'Yea, okay, fine.' Noah looked amused. 'Your profile said you do a lot of work representing less fortunate people in court.'

Austin nodded, happy for the change of pace.

'I tried studying law, so I'm kind of keen on social justice issues,' Noah continued. 'I dropped you a message hoping you would agree to meet for a hot drink based on that. Like that was the sub-text or whatever you want to call it. But I think it is fair to say I'd be lying if I said I didn't think your profile pic was alluring.'

The way the last word — *alluring* — was said, as well as Noah's awkward sentence construction, gave Austin pause. It indeed became clear to him within the span of a few minutes that there was no easy collaboration between Noah's interests and his own, and ordinarily that would have — or should have — been the end of it. They'd make small talk whilst finishing off their coffees and head their separate ways, likely to never speak again. But Noah kept talking past the first cup of coffee, and then past a second and third. And now Austin felt stuck in.

'Right, so to answer your question,' he said after growing comfortable enough to return to Noah's initial line of inquiry. 'The obvious: I'm a white man, middle-class. Mum's American, father was a Brit. But those descriptors don't say much and don't express how I feel. I mean, those are only the immutable characteristics that shape who I am because of what I'm around or how I was born. This society we live in shapes our identity, you know, in the same way that being mixed race would shape your identity, I'd guess.'

Austin sounded a bit pompous, and he stopped to take stock of his date's reaction.

But Noah wasn't fazed. 'Go on,' he simply said. But before Austin could, Noah got up and went to the loo.

'Sorry,' he said returning to the table, 'I drank a lot of fluids today.'

Austin said it was no problem and tried to get back on track with his thoughts.

'I think what I'm trying to say is that it's not easy to put into a few adjectives how I define myself. I define myself in relation to others — all human beings do — but I also think that to know oneself takes years of practice.'

Noah's eyebrows raised.

'Working on yourself, understanding what you want, where you are, your limitations and your strengths — that sort of thing. Humans are often faced with competing alternatives: we are vulnerable and emotional beings.'

This sort of talk often met Austin with the confused looks of dead-eyed colleagues, accustomed to hearing another of his quasi-academic monologues. But Noah only sat there, still vaguely amused.

Emboldened by not having been interrupted yet, Austin continued, 'In one of my favourite books, *Mrs Dalloway*, the husband of this titular Clarissa Dalloway buys his wife some flowers and he thinks up how he's going to give them to her and tell her that he loves her. But when he gets home, Richard — that's what he's called — is unable to get the words out. I felt let down the first time I read it, ashamed for him and sorry for her. But then the script is flipped because Clarissa takes the flowers and knows what Richard means without his saying it. It's the perfect unity of thought and deed that creates real identity; it is a moment of true vision.'

Austin had begun to ramble — to 'wax philosophical' as his mother would call it — so he stopped. Noticing Noah was somewhat taken aback, he asked, 'What about you? How do you identify?'

Noah sat still for a moment and then said, 'I've thought a lot about how I identify, and I've decided that I don't. Not in some "I don't do labels" way but in a sort-of "I'm complex and can't choose any easy descriptors" kind-of way.' He uttered each word, taking time to think over any future consequence.

Austin's pulse shot through this throat. 'So, I've spilled my guts and fought for the right words, for you to say that?!'

Noah smiled, nonplussed. 'And what about sexuality?'

'Oh.' Austin's turn to be taken aback by the frankness of the question.

Noah smirked. 'It's not a test.'

'Of course, it's not, I just don't find this is something most Muslims want to talk about.'

'And you're assuming I'm a Muslim?' Noah retorted, making Austin realise his earlier comment about Noah being of mixed race hadn't been ignored or forgotten.

'Well your surname is Hakim, for starters, so I'm pretty sure you've got Arab parents, right?' He treaded lightly now and stared down at his coffee mug as though the brown liquid held answers.

Noah's mouth begun to turn down and Austin thought he'd gone too far when Noah said, 'So that makes me a Muslim because I've got a Bengali father?' It was a self-effacing statement. The dramatic turn on Noah's face gave him away.

'Sorry, I didn't mean any offence, it was only a supposition, a guess —'

'No offence taken, man. As a matter of fact, I am Muslim, or I was raised one, but I'm not practicing, not in any real way. I believe in Allah and I follow the ethical guidelines. But in any case, I want to get back to the question at hand. What's your sexual preference?'

'This is a call to self-reflection,' Austin said. His eyes darted into the space beyond his interlocutor's head.

'Why's it so difficult for you to answer the question, mate?'

Mate?! thought Austin. 'It's not difficult. But it is a very direct thing to ask and I'm trying to choose my words carefully.' He could see from Noah's face he wasn't going to back down. 'Sexuality is not a black-and-white thing, you see. I could say simply I'm gay but that's not the best way to describe who I find attractive. I've been in relationships with men and women but prefer men these days. Though I know they are more trouble.'

This was not altogether true. Austin found a girl attractive, once, when he was nineteen and very drunk at a university house party. Ever since, he fancied himself something of a bisexual. It became a convenient way to dodge questions of this variety.

Noah laughed. 'Are they now?'

'Absolutely. My experience. What I want to say is to deal with oneself and with the challenges to self-identity is a prerequisite for any sort of meaningful relationship.'

He had used this line a dozen times, always on the back of the bisexual bit.

'Even friendships?' Noah asked, more to the air than to Austin.

'Yes, even friendships. If I don't know myself, how can anybody else know me?'

'Sometimes another person can know you better than you know yourself. My mother used to say to me: "I know you better than you know yourself, Noah."'

Recalling his own mother, Austin smiled. She would say nearly the exact same words every time he would catch a cold but pretend to be alright so that he could play with his neighbourhood friends. 'Sure, I think most kids hear that from their parents at one point or another.'

'So,' Noah asked, 'doesn't that negate your point?'

Despite the sudden wave of nostalgia over what he perceived as a less-than-happy childhood, Austin gave a coy smile. 'Maybe on some level it does. How much do our parents know us though? Sure, they know the basic things we need for survival as children and perhaps they are in touch with our material needs or wants up until a certain age. They know what toys we want or what cartoons we like watching on TV. What do your mother or father know about you now, though? My mother has no idea what I do for a living, what my hobbies are, or anything else meaningful. I don't bring these things up and she doesn't ask. If you go ask her now, maybe she would say she knows me, but she doesn't, not in truth.'

The reality of Austin's adolescence returned to him. His insides coiled into a ball made of rubber bands, bouncy but with little elasticity.

Meanwhile, Noah took a moment to think things over as his mouth turned slightly downwards. 'And what you are saying is the relationship with your mum is superficial?'

'This conversation is getting off topic, isn't it?' Noah's expression remained unchanged, so Austin continued: 'Well umm, yes, it is superficial but it's also indicative of what I said earlier about knowing yourself before you can know others — I don't desire that kind of deep relationship with my mother, so I don't let her in, don't explain to her or let her see the "real" me.'

Beginning to get nostalgic over his own upbringing, Noah countered, solemnly, 'Muslims are supposed to respect their parents above all else.'

Austin's mental images fast forwarded to his university philosophy class on world religions. He could picture the lecturer, his long scraggly beard and ruffled suit, every bit appearing the part of the hippie socialist he professed to be. He remembered this lecturer challenging the only burqa-wearing student in the class; how he felt sorry for her at the time. Not because she was being attacked for her religion, something she had more-or-less no choice over, being only eighteen and a first-year undergraduate recently moved out of her parents' home and into the dorms, but because he knew what it was like to not be able to change some essential part of who you are.

Thinking of his classmate, Austin replied, 'I'm sure there are many Muslims who believe that, yes ... Look, I've not turned my back on my mother, but I keep her very much at a distance.'

They carried on talking about relationships with parents and knowing oneself in relation to others for several more minutes before Noah excused himself to use the loo again. Austin was glad for the break in talking, as he felt most of the weight for carrying the conversation sat on his shoulders. He tried using those few minutes to make sense of what was happening. A coffee date turned into a dialogue on identity, ranging from race to sexuality and relationships. He welcomed this level of conversation, not often finding someone he connected with on a philosophical or academic level, but he also wondered about motivation — Noah's and his own. It didn't take more than a few minutes for Austin to put a deceptively simple label on his feelings for Noah: love. This was love. As cliché and improbable as it sounded in his head, Austin sensed a deep bond with Noah that intensified precisely because he was asking these deep questions mere minutes after meeting. It was too much for Austin's cup-half-empty mind to expect Noah to feel the same way, or to label it as such, but one question floated across his mind repeatedly that afternoon: Is Noah attracted to me in any way?

That night, Austin dreamed he was flying. He recorded the memory in his notebook the next morning.

My arms move like I am swimming, but swimming through air. Flying is not easy, I put effort into it, but I manage to lift from the ground and pass over buildings and trees. Everything is beautiful. The things about London I ordinarily find ugly have new life, such colour. I see the grey smog and revel in its ability to mask the harshness of the pavement running in all directions. I notice the very top spire of St Paul's, its clear and defined tiers of masonry. I see my mother. She smiles from the steps of the church. Her hair floats in the breeze. Such potential realised. It was brilliant. Sad to wake up today.

A recurring dream; he could recall having it as early as ten or eleven years old. The dream, its vividness and its strength, was something he connected with his mother. Where other children took pride in the professions of their parents, he took pride in his mother's appearance, especially her lovely long hair. Is your mum coming to pick you up today? He heard his teachers ask this many times, as they too propelled toward the magnetism of Millicent Smith, once even asking her to remove the pins from her hair so they could see the well-kept mane. But when she cut it off a few years later, everything snapped. His mother's magnanimity was inexplicably linked to the length of her hair. When it became short, no one paid her any mind and she became like all the other mothers. Austin resented her for it. And the dreaming began.

The British royal family are legendary hunters. So culturally and economically important was their taste for the kill that eight Royal Parks were built within London alone to accommodate this proclivity. Beginning with Greenwich Park in 1427, these 4,900 acres became the domain of king and kingdom until with the increasing urbanisation of London, they were preserved as freely accessible open space and were converted to public parks in the 19th century.

It is The Regent's Park, first opened to the general public in 1835, which most impressed Austin. The south, east, and most of the west side are lined with elegant white stucco terraced houses. Streaming through the northern end of the park is Regent's Canal, an artificial waterway so breathtaking Austin could imagine he was in Venice or Amsterdam and not murky Northwest London. He knew this park with its lowly gardens and high-reaching hills well. It's where he ran twice a week, three if he could find the physiological petrol.

Running up Primrose Hill with its lush edges and clear rounded skyline, Austin grew tired and lost the will to do another kilometre. He didn't feel like nodding his head to the beat pounding through his wireless earphones, an involuntary tick whenever he ran, his feet and head connecting in one rhythmical stroke. Finally, he gave up. Descending the hill at a slow pace, he noticed with agitation he was being watched. More than watched, stared at. By an older man who had made for himself a pallet of old blankets on a grassy part of the downward slope. Austin thought at first the man was homeless. His top was a tatty tartan and his shorts looked like they'd been cut with scissors and came up too high on his thighs so that bits of his butt cheeks peeked out if he moved even a little. Austin hated to see this. Homeless people not taken care of. Though he could never work out if the disdain he felt was directed to the government, with their clear and ignored responsibility to do more, or if it was a blame he assigned to the homeless themselves. Austin thought all this while still breathing heavily when the man called to him.

'Hello there —'

These words were crisp, almost melodic. Austin glanced in the man's direction and then immediately regretted doing so.

'— Yes, you there.'

Austin took out his earphones and folded them into the pocket of his running shorts. 'Excuse me?'

After all that staring and calling out, you would imagine the man, who Austin could see now was not wearing any ordinary tartan but in fact donned Burberry, would have something important or at least interesting to say.

'I said, "hello there" and I meant to follow it up with a hearty how are you ...'

Memory can play tricks on you. And this is ever truer when one is exhausted from running seven and a half kilometres around and up and down the expanse of Regent's Park on an unusually warm Saturday morning. Consequently, Austin put his head down for a moment and wondered if he knew this man. A former client? Maybe an old mate from school? He didn't want to be rude. He fiddled with the listening device through the pocket of his shorts and then reached for his iPhone, a nervous tick. It must have appeared as though he were preparing to walk away when the man spoke again.

'... I only wondered how you are. That's all.'

'I'm fine, thank you. Just fine.' And then, tucking his hands into his pockets: 'Do I know you? I'm sorry my memory is —'

'No, we don't know one another. Yet.' The man stood up. His denim shorts were more precariously short than they first appeared. Apart from his behind, his considerable manhood hung in the visible balance between his rip-cut jeans and thighs.

'I'm sorry,' Austin said, with typical regret. The readiness of the English to apologise for something they haven't done is remarkable. 'I'm not getting you.'

The man took two steps closer now. 'Come sit down. I feel sure we will be on better terms soon.'

The earphones found their way back into Austin's head then and he turned to walk away.

'No, don't go,' the man called out. He took another three steps forward and latched gently onto Austin's forearm.

Austin shook the man's hand loose. 'Hey, I don't know what you're on about.'

The man sat down now. Anxiety covered his face. 'You look so fit, I thought we could get to know one another. Let's see what we can get into this afternoon.'

The thought of looking fit made Austin smile but this was soon replaced with repugnance. This was not how you went about getting someone's attention. It felt dirty.

'Mm, well, sorry,' he said, 'I'm on my way home.' He started off again and then turned and called to the man behind, to be sure things were clear: 'No, you cannot come with me.'

A tiny rush of wind greeted him as he turned the key into flat 83. The balcony doors had been left ajar. There was a little bit of genius in this oversight. The gust had a refreshing effect on Austin, which he much needed after an arduous run and a run-in with the pervert on Primrose Hill. As he stripped off his sweaty clothes and stepped into the shower, he tilted his head up and let a little of the water into his mouth. He felt more alive these days, and it was all thanks to Noah, or rather to that surprisingly enjoyable first date. Austin marvelled at how much transformation could take place in forty-eight hours. You can go from cynic to Pollyanna. The change could even be noticed in his appreciation of Abbey Road which he could see by straining his neck out the small window on the wall behind the shower and down the five floors below. The road was no longer the threat he always imagined it to be, replete as it was with tourists waiting in queue to make silly motions on the famous zebra crossing.

He smiled when he saw them now and felt lucky to live on such a historic thoroughfare.

Good moods always precipitated action in Austin. Whether this was because he found himself in a good mood so rarely these days or because he was the 'man of action' his tutors and colleagues always claimed he was proved immaterial. He would do it now. He would make the next move.

Reaching for his mobile phone, he sent Noah a message.

> -- Hey there. Would you be up for meeting again? X

> -- Yea, sounds good.

This hadn't been the raving with excitement response he hoped for. In the recesses of his mind, Austin expected Noah to write back some undying confession of love ... or at least respond with more than three syllables.

> -- I mean, only if you are sure ...

> -- I feel like, you know, getting to know you.

Austin knew! But thought, 'play it cool.'

> -- I'd love to get know more of you as well.

-- Tomorrow evening? There's a bar in Bloomsbury ...

Oh, I'm so glad, he thought and practically smiled his face off. He sat in silence for a moment, letting the breeze do the work of filling the dead space with subtle noise. When the gale calmed, he turned on the television and began flicking through Netflix. He stopped on a cover image of two boys staring into each other's eyes with what could only be described as lust. One boy was white and the other had a lovely brown complexion reeking of exoticism. It wasn't hard for Austin to imagine himself and Noah as these two chaps engaged in a soft, playful romance precipitated perhaps secretly at first and growing in depth and magnitude over time. As the preview played on, the camera panned to a violent eruption between the boys and cut back again to a sex scene bordering on soft porn. The final scene showed the boys as men, walking hand-in-hand down a long country road. It reminded him of a line from a poem: *There is such a shelter in each other.*

It had been a fine afternoon.

The dream of many an aspiring barrister is to secure a pupillage at a top commercial chambers in the City. Others aspire to the criminal sets in Chancery Lane. Docklands Chambers found itself at an odd impasse between the two: a criminal law firm in Canary Wharf. This was one of the new-fangled chambers aimed to 'serve the people where they are'. One presumed this meant the various criminal doers in the whole of East London and not in the comparatively wealthy Docklands. As a contemporary outfit, its founding partners wanted contemporary ways of doing things. There was to be a fancy coffee machine in the kitchen to make all sorts of cortados and macchiatos and café au laits. There was a childcare centre on site. Dry cleaning was complementary. And Monday morning all-staff meetings were held in the Living Room, a dense space masking the ample amounts of sunlight it received by walls lined with hardbound legal volumes and the occasional GQ or Elle magazine tossed on a table. Everyone wondered who read these; no one ever claimed responsibility. It was understood that the magazines were there for aesthetic. Austin tossed one of them to the side as he sat in a faux-leather covered swivel chair at the long, glass-top conference table.

The trick to surviving these Monday morning gatherings was to arrive early. If you could claim a seat near the door, you might have the chance to sneak out after you gave your list of weekly goals and before Montague, the senior partner who had recently made Queen's Counsel, made his traditional pep talk on what a great firm this was, how they were privileged to be helping the under-privileged, and how it made good economic sense to do so even if their own individual pockets were lined less handsomely than their peers in Holborn or Liverpool Street. Austin believed in all these things, though not as fervently as he might once have done. He just didn't need to hear it repeated week after week.

By the time his colleagues arrived, Austin had been staking his claim to an exit-row seat for the better part of fifteen minutes. The pupils filed in first, eager to be seen as proactive, and then came the QCs, as eager but for different reasons, and finally the lot in the middle, people at the same rank and file as Austin but with less ambition to get out early. As the juniors began their weekly reports — which were more like to-do lists than statements of achievement — Austin focused his attention on his MacBook, cleverly propped in front of him at such an angle the screen could not be made out from any direction. Another benefit of seats near the door was no one sat behind you. With his next date looming in, he checked his watch — nine hours and thirty-two minutes to prepare for what he imagined would be another hard intellectual conversation.

It was somewhere amongst reading the morning papers, browsing CNN, and scrolling through his Twitter feed that Montague called on him. Had Austin been paying attention, he would have heard this:

'There are,' said Montague QC bringing his hands together, 'a myriad of reasons why we need to expand further our reach into the community ... I suppose it would be better to say we must *re-position* ourselves as a top-quality provider of criminal legal services to those that cannot afford the other chambers but whose own government — yes, the same government in our own Westminster — have let down by not providing access to public defence ...'

Under other conditions, if Montague did not sound so damn rehearsed, he might have been quicker to catch Austin's attention.

'... 31.1 crimes committed per annum per one thousand people in East London. That is 104% of the national crime rate. And so, to conclude' — everyone sighed with gratitude at the rounding down — 'Docklands Chambers will start taking on more briefs of underrepresented persons and our very own rising star Austin will be our man to handle the first of these cases.'

The applauding snapped Austin out of digital limbo.

'Congrats, Austin!' said the colleague sat nearest.

Austin screeched. 'Huh?'

'... This first client's brief will be delivered by her solicitor this very afternoon,' Montague went on saying.

Austin checked his watch again right before getting off the underground near Bloomsbury. He felt self-conscious, but the rabid preparation took the edge off and went some way to putting him more in the know. Had he been able to articulate this anxiety, he might have wondered if Noah were his match, someone who could relate to the sheer angst of getting by, day-in and day-out. There might have been something comforting in that.

But sat on the tube that afternoon, his new client, the first fortunate of the many unfortunates, as Montague later called them, whose cases Austin would now be handling, came to mind. Olivia had been charged with attempted murder for a second time in as many decades. She told him when she went to prison on the first charge, she was naturally petrified she wouldn't survive. A few months into her fifteen-year sentence though, Olivia said she began to bond with the other inmates, particularly those also locked up on some variant of an attempted murder charge. On her account, they all related to one another not because they committed the same crimes, but out of a knowledge they *could* commit a crime and, in some ways, get away with it. Yes, they'd been sent to prison, but they'd succeeded in not only stopping short of actually killing someone — that required quite a lot of willpower in her estimation — but also in scaring their victims and the victims' families and friends. They had gotten close enough to gain someone's trust, nearly murder the person, and still serve a light sentence. The best of both worlds, she called it. Apparently, the best of both worlds was something Olivia needed to experience twice in life. In the minutes between the tube stops of Holborn and Russell Square, Austin wondered if he was but some adaptation of this bullshitter, scraping his way from day to week to month impressing people with rubbish facts and academic speak. Attempting to murder them with words.

Noah arrived at three o'clock and greeted Austin with a hug instead of a hand shake as he'd done on their first meeting. The hug deepened his affection toward Noah and despite Austin's apprehension about coming off like a less-monstrous version of his newest client, the physical embrace made him want to leap straight into regurgitating the jargon crammed in his head all morning, if only to impress Noah with how up to speed he was on the day's breaking news.

After ordering a beer in the empty bar, Noah asked, 'So what's new?'

Austin wanted to play it cool but couldn't hold the overload of media spinning in his head. He sprang into a monologue on Clinton's new book, the effects of global warming, and the value of the pound all fused into a five-minute rant.

Noah wasn't impressed. 'Yea actually I'm asking about you. What's new with *you*?'

This guy's radar is keen, thought Austin. He remembered a line he'd read or heard somewhere. *The first step of change is becoming aware of your own bullshit.* Austin believed, on a very basic level, he was the kind of person who always looks for things to go wrong and he kept little phrases like this tucked in the back of his cranium as forms of self-care. It was an insecurity that led to his tendency to fill dead conversational space with rehearsed jargon, plastering over empty spaces like a Band-Aid. He would inevitably blame himself when the listener was unreceptive, but never had anyone stopped him in his tracks with so much force, not in the way Noah did. He needed a different approach, one that didn't try to make academic that which was supposed to be heartfelt. Still, Noah didn't strike Austin as brainy or even articulate, but this was not bad. He was rather like someone he'd known for many years who still has a mystique about them. This was all rather promising.

'Okay, so this past Friday,' Austin began, 'I accompanied a colleague and sometime-friend Rachael to pick up her children from school in the suburbs north of London. We drove first to the nursery where her three-year-old waited anxiously for us behind a chain fence with a small mass of other toddlers. I sat in the passenger seat of the SUV while Rachael swooped in to collect her little girl who, like the other children — all prisoners waiting to be set free — were joyous to be collected by their mothers and subsequently buckled into car seats, strapped into another sort of jail. A few miles down the two-lane road, we arrived at the grammar school where Rachael's twelve-year-old boy studied. The routine here was different. A buddy system of mums and other caregivers created a hierarchy on the playground where we waited for the children to emerge from the school's front doors. Yummy mummies in their high heels and too-much makeup huddled near the lamppost. Fashionable, younger mums with their Stan Smith sneakers and designer handbags formed their own clique opposite. A third group, where I found myself with Rachael, consisted of a hodgepodge of worn-out looking mothers and the occasional father. Here gathered working parents and people in their late thirties and early forties, perhaps having decided to start families later in life. The conversation veered from however so-and-so's son performed in his subjects to discussing the fashion missteps of the yummy mummies and the snobbery of the Stan Smithers. At half three the young boys straggled out of the school doors, many of them looking much less excited to be leaving school than did the toddlers on our previous stop. These boys, unlike their caregivers, had no sense of the social boundaries and taboos I found myself surrounded by only moments before. Rachael's son was chummy with one of the Stan Smither's kids and as the mothers exchanged murmured pleasantries, I noticed another student around the same age as Rachael's son being held by the hand by a rather young-looking man with no noticeable resemblance to the child.'

Recalling this now, Austin froze in panic exactly as he'd done on the Friday when he accompanied Rachael. The man. The kid. It reminded him of nightmare that had frightened him on more than one occasion. He wanted to shout, to alert someone to stop this man not more than a teenager from kidnapping this boy. Couldn't they get out of their petty cliques and forced pleasantries to see what was happening before their eyes?! But no, it was a dream. Not real.

He kept this part of the incident to himself and continued to Noah: 'Rachael tapped me on the shoulder. "See that one?" she says pointing to the same young man with the little boy in his hand, "He's the nanny of the Johnson family." "Oh yea," the Stan Smith mum chimes in sarcastically, "You get a lot of gay help up this way. Not exactly safe if you ask me. People should take care of their own kids." Rachael nodded her head. This was one thing all the mums could agree on — whether related to sexual orientation or outsourcing the care of the children to a third-party, I don't know. I just know it didn't feel right.'

Austin looked up, the bar was full now, and he became suddenly aware he'd been in something of a trance, his memory of the encounter felt jumbled and although he thought he knew what it meant to be marginalised, even if not deliberately by those women on the school grounds, the vividness thrusting itself in the midst of the retelling was unexpected. He had tears in the corners of his eyes. He recognised the emotion, but he could not remember having experienced it before and therefore did not know what to call it.

The stream of consciousness spewing from Austin's mouth was too much for his date. It wasn't long before Noah made his excuses and left Austin there alone with his glass of white wine and clouded memory.

Taking his journal from his briefcase, Austin opened to a blank page. In big letters, he wrote: *What now?*

Self-induced dissociative identify disorder. Austin surmised Noah's diagnosis, fancying himself some kind of modern-day Freud as he finished off the pinot grigio. Noah possessed the rare quality of being able to completely reassure you on first encounter and completely throw you just when he's made you feel on solid ground since he's 'like everyone else.' But DID, what psychiatrists now call multiple personality disorder, wasn't quite right. Noah did exhibit a certain brand of split personality, not simultaneously but subsequently. First soothing and cool, and then disarming. But disarmament can be ever so enchanting. His disarming smile; his disarming wit;

his disarming logic. All clichés and not a one of them untrue. Not in Austin's mind.

There is particular kind of foolish naivety that comes with young love. Late the next day, Austin thought he might be depressed. Not classically depressed in the 'sense of loss of interest or pleasure, feelings of guilt or low self-worth' definition but more in the disturbed sleep, low appetite, low energy, and poor concentration realm of depression. Often able to identify these symptoms in other people, including his mother, he always thought he was somehow immune. The diagnoser not the diagnosed. But there they appeared — all the tell-tale signs.

He sat in his office cubicle and looked out at the windows at a sheath of concrete and steel dotting the horizon. The eyes were the problem. Noah wore these honey-suckle pupils that pierced deep. Chips of ice threatening to cut away all your self-defence mechanisms. The depression sat in earlier in the day when he began thinking he might never hear from Noah again. There was something quite definitive about the way they left things the previous afternoon. And with no follow-up phone call or text since, Austin felt anxious and hopeful, defeated and nervous all at once.

Is this love? Still a stranger to meaningful relationships at thirty-four years old, and who could blame him? Positive role models were scarce. 65% of his firm were male, and of that 71% were either divorced or single and the other odd quarter spent more time in the office than with their partners. He picked up his iPhone and scrolled through his Instagram feed. It was his only real means of keeping up some semblance of communication with the outside world. A quick glance of the latest posts showed Thomas87 holidaying in the Maldives, apparently without his wife, ItsMeRobin visiting her parents up north, still single and probably lesbian, and DocChris posting stories from his clinical rotations, which to Austin was emblematic of his generation and social class: work hard, play never.

Gritting his teeth, Austin stared at the carpeted grey walls of his cubicle. Sometimes these moments of clarity would manifest where the outside world showed itself as banal, a longing for something more. But like on this afternoon, those moments would hasten more depressing feelings. What did he expect to happen? Noah was six years his junior, and while that wasn't a huge age gap, Austin felt very strongly their differences would push Noah away. But push him away from what? A life filled almost entirely with a cycle of work-eat-sleep, repeat.

'Hey!' someone shouted from across the room, Austin looked up but on seeing who it was, he put his head down and pretended to concentrate on the pile of papers atop his desk.

'Oi, Austin!' The voice got nearer, and it became harder for Austin to pretend not to hear it.

At last the man reached his cubicle and tapped on Austin's shoulder.

'Oh, Nelson, hello,' said Austin finally looking up. The stunted cubicle walls began closing in.

Nelson was the obvious gay at Docklands Chambers. Every firm needs an obvious gay — the person, typically male, who embraces the very stereotypes of flamboyance and effeminacy melded into one. This is the gay all the men, Austin included, loved to hate and all the women couldn't help but love due mainly to his easily identifiable associations with the heterocentric mainstream. Think Jack MacFarland with a Mulberry bag. Nelson had a thing for Austin.

'Good day to you, Austin,' he beamed. 'I called your name a couple times, but I guess you were wrapped up in work.' Nelson leaned over to peak at the stack of papers on Austin's desk. 'It's busy these days, isn't it?'

'It is, it is ... did you, uh, want something?' Austin pushed the papers to one side so they were out of Nelson's sightline.

'Montague sent me over here to ask how you are getting on with the new client's case. Olivia something-or-other.'

'Montague sent you?' The implication was dubious at best.

Nelson bit on the ends of his fingers. 'Uh huh.'

'Why would the senior partner send *you* over here to check on *me*?'

'Well,' he shuffled back and forwards, 'I don't know. Maybe he is busy and doesn't have time to check himself?' Even Nelson was unsure of this explanation.

'Everything's fine, Nelson, just fine. In fact, I'm all done with the case. Settled with a plea.' Austin gave him a little gawk of offence. 'Anything else?'

'No, no, cheers for that,' he smiled, 'but may I say you look very dashing indeed today.'

Nelson turned and walked away, skipping as he went.

Austin returned to staring at the walls of his cubicle lit unnervingly with fluorescent light. Christ, I don't want to end up like that. He resolved then to make the next move, to do something to show Noah he was not the sort to wait around for the other person to call. Too much time had gone by and he'd be damned to repeat the same mistakes.

Austin opened WhatsApp. God, Noah's profile pic was hot. His legs twitched a bit as he typed.

> -- Thanks for yesterday afternoon ... I really like you xx

I really like you?! Am I bloody thirteen years old? He was embarrassed not to have spent more time composing the perfect message, one which would have been in equal measures masculine and im-pressionable.

He picked up the phone again to delete the message, but he saw then from the double blue check marks that Noah had already read it. Plop-ping his head on his desk, Austin let out a loud sigh.

Four hours later, Austin sat on the sofa with a Marks & Spencer ready meal. He ate the spaghetti bolognese and flicked the television between CNN and the BBC, trying to find something to catch his interest and take his mind off the message as yet gone unanswered.

With only a few drops of red sauce remaining in the plastic carton, Austin picked up the Molesk-ine journal.

Right now, I am powerless. I'm normally in control of my whole life. Meticulous with everything. And now, it all seems confused. How could I let a silly guy who is out of my league make me feel this way? It was two dates. I'm not sure you could call them dates, but I'm so out of practice at anything social that it felt like such a huge deal just to get some attention. I don't know what I'll do if he doesn't respond, which appears pretty likely. I suppose I'll just go back to normal. Work, takeaways, daffy mum, my one or two real friends. Is this middle age paranoia ...!

His phone buzzed then. The sound of an incoming text message was so rare it took Austin a moment to work out how to fetch the notification.

-- Sorry for the slow reply, was at work and the boss breathin down my neck. Would def be in for round 3 if you're up for it? X

Keeping secrets ran in Noah Hakim's family. In the way other families passed down blue eyes or a tendency toward diabetes, the Hakims were all co-conspirators. The ten-year-old Noah knew this when his mother told him Santa Claus has a naughty list, so you have to be on your best be-haviour. And the seventeen-year-old Noah knew it when Mo, his older cousin, refused to admit the pair shoplifted from Boots and instead said they watched someone else take the condoms. And now the twenty-eight-year-old Noah had repeated the same old Hakim pattern on this boy he met last week for coffee.

Only the circumstances were different this time. He could justify white lies about religion, race, social class, his proclivity toward the odd stimulant, but sexuality? Shittt. He was knackered just thinking about it.

And yet he *couldn't* stop. His face is like the moon, pale and mysterious. His hair has the shine of a young man, smooth honey dripping over the tips of his ears. I'm quite poetic, huh? Noah thought, impressed with himself, and then looked in the mirror and noticed his own premature wid-ow's peak matted down with pomade. It was Austin's body/mind combo which was most inter-esting. He met plenty of educated blokes roaming the clubs of East London. Most were artists or artist-wannabes, but few of them were successful and even fewer took care of themselves. (Bohemi-anism didn't need to mean not showering, did it?) Still, it hadn't stopped him from playing the field. Black girls, white guys, any sort of Arab, even that super-hot Chinese twink that fucked him last month. He went through them all. But Austin was the first one he'd caught feelings over in a long time.

With the mirror proving disappointing, Noah sat down on the sofa of his room, a space in varying stages of construction and deconstruction, mainly because Noah never took the time to do a proper clean, preferring instead to move piles of things from one side of the room to the other. He moved two or three piles now to find a ballpoint pen and a scrap of paper. So, it worked out to something like this, he scribbled:

Pros	Cons
Hot bod	Not Muslim?
Intelligent	Age?
Race?	Race?
	Parents!

He crumbled the paper into his hands and threw the biro across the floor. The thing about Hakim secrets were that they ate at their bearers until they were suppressed. Suppression took many forms. Uncle Graeme used fine French wine to bury his sorrows — he reckoned even the Prophet would approve of a Burgundy appellation. Mo indulged in wife-gathering, visiting Morocco at regular intervals to pick up another demi-princess for his haram.

Noah reached for his phone. It was half seven and he needed to get to his parents' flat for eight o'clock. There was still time. He felt for his coat and yanked off the long Zara tag, something he forgot to do after picking it up from Westfield Mall, his one sartorial indulgence this season. He took a small plastic bag from the pocket and poured its contents on the coffee table. He formed the glistening white sequins into a single line and snorted them, inhaling deeply.

The clock struck eight chimes, but the Hakims weren't ready for dinner yet. It was Ramadan which meant they couldn't eat until 20.08 on the dot. Those eight minutes — seven yesterday, nine tomorrow — were like agony as everyone's stomachs grumbled. So close to breaking fast but not quite time.

As the call to prayer rang out, Noah popped a date into his mouth, mouthed the words to the evening prayer, and dug into the chicken biryani his father spent a large portion of the afternoon preparing. Iftar always felt like Christmas to Noah, or at least how he imagined other people felt who celebrate Christmas: jolly spirits, words of encouragement, light-hearted moods. Every night without fail for the whole month, his family's iftar spread was grand, with both vegetarian and non-vegetarian dishes and a variety of juices and sherbets on offer. It was a time when all misdeeds and missteps were to be forgotten, if not altogether forgiven. Aashirbaad and Lilly, his father and mother, even turned a blind eye to their eldest son living on his own, rarely attending mosque, and still without a wife — at twenty-eight, Allah forbid!

For his part, Noah's habit of hanging round the family home long after the evening meal was finished only further added to his parents' belief (more of a hope) that he was tired of living the secular life and thus looking to reconnect to his roots. Most days, he asked Lilly to pack him a Tupperware container to take back home with him. She assumed that like all good Muslims, a religion to which she herself converted into some three decades ago, her son ate the leftovers at Suhoor, the predawn meal before the next day's fast. In reality, Noah divided it into an additional two sealable plastic bowls, deep-freezing both to defrost at a later date when money was sure to be tight and hunger high.

But this evening, Lilly's eldest looked distracted. What she thought might be a case of loneliness or discontentment now appeared to be more serious. He paid progressive attention to his mobile phone and less to his siblings, with which he once shared a big brother camaraderie.

'What's on your mind?' she asked now as Aashirbaad put a second helping of biryani on Noah's plate.

'Huh?' he said, looking up from the screen.

'I asked how you were.'

'Oh, fine, fine. Everything's fine.'

'You've been on that bloody phone the whole evening,' Aashirbaad chimed in. 'Your mother and myself are worried about you.'

Noah placed his mobile next to his dinner plate. 'Happy?'

Lilly shot him a look of the kind only mothers can give. It was the sort of look that lets children, even grown ones, know who is in charge. 'I really cannot wrap my head around what's happening. You've been so distracted today and yesterday too.'

Noah glared back at Lilly, and then took another bite of rice.

'You can talk to us,' his father offered.

Noah rarely spoke about his personal life, and when he did it was to comment on office politics or his eating habits, small talk that pleased his father's work-hard ethos and his mother's concern for his physical well-being. But tonight, they all felt there was something being left unsaid.

'It's just this whole Ramadan has me distracted,' Noah offered up in return.

'Oh, but you've always loved this time of year!' Lilly exclaimed. 'Eid is around the corner.'

'I have, I do,' he said, confused, 'but I've met someone, you see, so my mind is elsewhere.'

'Oh. My. Allah.' Lilly nearly shouted, one of her favourite things being to twist popular expressions she either heard the children saying or read on Facebook into Islamised phrases. 'What absolutely wonderful news!'

This wasn't the first time Noah thought about how he might come out to his parents. Part of him wanted to play on the bisexual aspects of things, passing his sudden interest in boys off as a phase. The more his feelings for Austin grew, though, the less chance there seemed to be of convincing them, his mother especially, to accept a man in place of the daughter she always wanted. Confronted with the choice now, Noah did what generations of Hakims have done. He lied. And he didn't feel guilty.

'Yea, she's great ...'

Aashirbaad patted his son on the back. 'Smashing news!' Adding after a few more pats: 'We will need to meet and approve of her, of course.'

'Don't be daft, dear. If Noah is happy, so are we!' Noah did his best to smile as his mother continued. 'Better late than never, I say, Alhamdulillah.'

The other children had, by now, left the dining table, so Noah sat in an awkward triangle between an overly-excited mother on one side, a sceptical but supportive father on the other, and his own shameless omission front and centre.

'You'll love her,' he said then. 'How 'bout I bring her round to iftar tomorrow?'

'Holy Toledo Muhammad, peace be upon him,' Lilly said, pleased at the confirmation her future daughter-in-law was a practicing Muslim.

Aashirbaad winced. 'Yes, do indeed, is what your mother means.'

That night, sat in his cramped studio flat, Noah popped open a Pabst Blue Ribbon and flicked through the Royal Docks Community School yearbook. This should be easy, he thought. He could remember only a handful of burqa-wearing girls in his year. Some of them would be married by now, but he thought he could figure out which ones. The more attractive, wealthier girls would have gotten all the offers for arranged marriages, and the working-class boys probably snapped up most of the semi-attractive working-class girls. It was the way the world worked. That left the uglier girls, and Noah had an idea just which one: Tiara Rose Mirza.

There she was, on page fifteen of the yearbook. Too much eyeshadow, bushy brows, a wonky smile, Burqa askew. This was the kind of girl sure to be single. In his more sociable high school days, Noah kept the phone numbers of all his mates, most of them from the Bengali crowd, in his mobile phone contacts. He still used that old iPhone 3G and was happy to find Tiara's digits stored there. Opening WhatsApp, he thought how incredibly barmy her name was, and was surprised to have never thought of it when they were in school. It would have made for great jokes, sounding less like a name and more of a shade of pink: dusty rose, brick rose, similarly Tiara Rose.

No looker a decade ago, Noah thought there was little chance of Tiara getting any better with time. This happened with fine wines and old cheeses, not with Bengali girls from East London. And yet when he met her the next evening outside Aldgate East station, he was surprised to see that she had matured quite well. And now more surprised to learn she was unattached. With a sculpted figure twine-thin, her waist cinched under a simple black dress.

'I got the stuff you want,' she said, approaching him.

'Yea, cool, and I'm going to pay you tops for it,' he said, motioning at her to put the small packet back in her bag, 'but first you gonna come with me, right?'

She nodded. 'First time a client ever asked me on a date.'

Her eyebrows arched atop her velvet forehead. Perfect, he thought, knowing his mother would be pleased.

The hem of his polo neck cut into his throat. His vest stuck to his chest and scratched at the fine hairs rooted to his thorax. His black jeans were the only element of this ensemble that had a comfortable fit. Looking at it from the outside, the only clue to his uneasiness was Austin pulling the fabric of several layers of top away from his skin.

Zara leaned over the hob. In her tiny studio flat, she almost stood over him as she did this. He winced a little each time the water began to boil out from the pot. Not that Zara noticed. She happily stirred as he noticed the way she pulled her blonde locks back into a loose bun, just the way his mother did it. But this was not an altogether pleasant memory.

'You really ought to have told me about him earlier,' she said, turning from the cooktop. Her tone carried a certain gravity of disappointment.

'I know ... but what can I say?' He picked up his black coffee and took a sip, happy to return to creature comforts — this unadorned cup of java, familiar conversation with an old friend in whose flat he spent countless lazy afternoons. 'It's not like I fall into relationships every day.'

'Ha! You *never* fall into relationships.' He looks slightly unnerved today, she thought, knowing him as one does know the people you see most often. There was a touch of melancholy about him masked behind a Louis Vuitton scarf and Gucci loafers, some youngish male version of a lady who lunches.

In the years since Nottingham University, where they both read philosophy, Zara saw Austin in precisely zero relationships. The closest he got, as far as she knew, was a regretful one-night-stand six years ago with a Brazilian named Antonio who they met on an unplanned night out in Soho (Zara's idea). Antonio had been everything Austin never thought he could get his hands on: six-pack abs, a thickly exotic accent, and one hell of a bushy chest. And after a single taste of Antonio's elixir, he wanted more, which was exactly what Antonio, being both closeted and a tourist, was trying to avoid. It didn't help, though, that Tonio ('You call me Tonio, kk gatinho?') left his mobile number 'just in case'. That night, and more realistically the forty-eight hours Austin spent in vain hoping to get a response to a series of text messages, spiralled him into a fifteen-day, fourteen-night depression.

But grace is a spectator event. And it was largely thanks to Antonio, and to a short roll call of other men, primarily met online, that Austin's mind worked in a series of rules. Those pertaining to relationships included — Rule no. 1: Self-preservation. Rule no. 2: Be open and honest. Rule no. 3: Rule 2 only applies if you'll be neither hurt nor used. This summed it up to one rule, The Golden Rule: Never trust too quickly.

Zara stirred the red sauce in another pan on the hob. It was Austin's job to watch the spaghetti, making sure it ended up somewhere between too hard and overdone. Seeing the pot boil over on the electric burner, he reckoned he made a right mess of it already.

'Oh dear!' said Zara turning her attention to Austin's side of the cooktop. 'Pasta cooked *al dente* has a lower glycemic index than pasta that is cooked soft.'

Austin shook his head, wondering when her latest health kick started her caring about things like glycemic indices. 'Deliveroo?' he offered.

'Try being less facetious.'

'Okay ... so no food delivery then ...'

She reached for the kitchen drawer nearest her left-hand and pulled it open. Out tumbled an assortment of Asian takeaway menus and Pizza Hut coupons.

'I mean about men, darling,' she said, scanning a leaflet from Chin's Chinese.

'Sorry ... I didn't realise we were still on that. Men. ... I mean, the spaghetti?'

Most of the water boiled out of the pot. A clump of yellow-white noodles coalesced in the middle of the stainless steel.

'Oh, I don't really care about the pasta,' Zara said and picked up her phone. 'I'll get us prawn fried rice and spring rolls.'

There goes the trendy fad, thought Austin. After she placed the order, Zara sat at the table in her small kitchen-diner and poured him a glass of red wine. He could see the price tag had been peeled off, tiny sticky bits of residue of the discount sticker remained.

'How did you come by this one exactly?'

'His name is Noah. He's a man, not a thing, right? ... We met on a sort-of blind date.'

She smiled. 'Tinder is not a blind date, Aus.'

Austin explained their first meeting now, going into excruciating detail, so much so that he hurried past the intervening days of silence, pretending as though their two dates happened end-on-end. It seemed wrong to let Zara in on all his apprehension when, by all accounts, things were looking up. Maybe Noah would be the guy to help him throw the rulebook out the window. And anyway, relationships are not, he thought, what they *are* but how they *feel*. And right now, he felt pretty damn good about Noah Hakim.

Lilly Hakim wrapped her hair so eloquently in the aqua-marine taffeta burqa that Aashirbaad at first did not recognise his wife as she strode down the stairs of their terraced house. For a moment, he thought Sheikha Moza herself had somehow transmuted into a one-night temporary replacement spouse. When it dawned on him that it was indeed the fifty-eight-year-old woman he'd been in holy matrimony with for three decades, he gasped in excitement. It wasn't that Aashirbaad ordinarily found Lilly unattractive, but he was grateful for the handful of times each year where she made an extra effort to look the part. The wives of the other men on the local mosque council were all a bit homely, he had to admit, but he wanted to make a certain kind of impression on the lot of them as they came around for the Hakim Eid celebration that evening.

'You look lovely, dear.'

'Why thank you. Mash'Allah.'

Lilly was glowing. She too longed to show off to the other wives and, secretly, to the husbands. Ever since Aashirbaad was elected treasurer of the mosque last winter, she felt both a renewed sense of what it means to be Muslima — duty, honour, respect — and a sense of having all eyes on her. Why shouldn't the other men lust after her? In fact, since her husband stopped caring much for physical intimacy five years ago, just after the birth of their third son, Lilly relished the attention. He got his heir, a spare, and a back-up; job done. She would confess, though, a certain *je ne sais quoi* about him tonight, dressed as his was in a fresh thobe of pure white and a sleek red-checked headpiece.

'You look handsome too, darling.'

He winked and when he did, Lilly almost crumbled under the weight of his long eyelashes, almost too soft for a man his age.

Aashirbaad mumbled some response. God, I hope she keeps the flirting to a minimum tonight, he thought, and turned to walk back to his study, directly opposite the kitchen, one room off each side of the house's central corridor. The truth was Aashirbaad was distracted with a problem bigger than his wife's looks, namely his eldest son.

Tiara Rose had been pleasant enough when she visited the other night for iftar, but there was something quite distracting about her mannerism. It was, in a word, fidgety. She looked uncomfortable merely being there. Despite all evidence to the contrary, Aashirbaad was a man of tradition. It was true he did not have the arranged marriage his own parents had hoped for, choosing instead to wed the only Irish Catholic girl in his otherwise all-brown enclave of Northeast London. But it was also true that as exotic a choice as Lilly had been, she'd also been a sensible option, her reputation (or lack thereof) spotless. It had been, in the end, almost a celebration: Aashirbaad would marry a white girl, one with no ill history to speak-of, the child of immigrants like himself, and she would convert. They were to be the perfect example of the power of Islam to change lives and build inter-cultural bridges. All of this had worked, at least for appearance sake, the last thirty years, but his eldest son chasing after a girl called Tiara Rose was but a step too far. Her reputation, it had to be said, preceded her and there was little doubt, thought Aashirbaad, a girl with that kind of name, wearing her uncovered hair in that sort-of style, was single. And it would be over his dead body for Noah to be the one to change that.

'Lilly!' he called out from his study, leaning out from the rolling chair lodged in front of an old particleboard desk, 'We need to talk about Noah ...'

Lilly picked up the phone extension in the kitchen to ring her son. I swear to Allah we are the only household in England still with a landline, she thought, as she punched in the digits to Noah's mobile. As the line ringed, she stared at the dated lacquered green cabinetry and resolved to keep the kitchen door closed when the guests arrived.

'Your father and I have been thinking,' she began without a proper greeting as Noah answered, 'you should bring that lovely young lady ... Tiara, was it? ... round here for the Eid party tonight.' This was in, in fact, not precisely what Aashirbaad and Lilly discussed, but a woman dressed to the nines can be awfully persuading. Let's just get to know the girl, she offered, and Aashirbaad came to see it as an opportunity to dig a little deeper into Tiara Rose's hazy past.

Now this put Noah into a dilemma. Not only because (1) he had no intentions of marrying Tiara Rose or parading her around for his father's masjid friends to gossip over, and (2) he anyway had snubbed her and her numerous text messages since their after-iftar shag.

'Yea, I'm uhhh not sure that's such a good idea, mum.'

The whole idea of the family Eid celebration got Noah worked up. What had once been his own version of holiday cheer that he could talk up when everyone else focused on mince pies and Santa Claus coming down the chimney had been turned into a little bit of Jahannam, complete with ultraconservative mosque-goers ('We haven't seen you lately at Jummah'), their children (some of them beautiful boys he couldn't dare engage with), and an utter lack of anything resembling family camaraderie. It was all about appearances now.

'You see,' he said, 'I think Tiara Rose has plans with her own fam tonight.'

'Yes, yes, of course. Well then ...' and as Lilly made to hang-up the last remaining landline phone in all of Northeast London, Noah Hakim got an idea.

'Why don't I bring my mate instead? Lovely chap, a solicitor, I think he's real interested in Islam and all.'

Now if there was anything more exciting to Lilly than displaying her version of Eid to the local mosque council and their families, replete as it was with her fine china set decorated with little hollies and berries (a hold-over from her Catholic days), it was the idea of a potential convert descending upon the Hakim family. Someone like herself, both in temperament and colour, though she wouldn't acknowledge this latter bit out loud.

Lilly's heart pounded a little faster each time the brass knocker on the front door pounded and it regained its composure each time she was disappointed to find it was the council president or vice-president or a member-at-large, all people she'd only thirty-five minutes ago been eager to impress. By the time the fourth set of guests arrived, Lilly retreated to the marital bedroom on the upper floor to reapply her eyeshadow and spray a generous heap of Chanel No 5 all over her body. She knew it to be frivolous — the perfume had been a gift from Aashirbaad three anniversaries ago and she'd rationed it ever since — but her nerves were getting the best of her. The complex blend of rose, jasmine, and iris layered over a warm base of sandalwood, vanilla, and amber created a soothing effect. She heard the knocker pound a fifth time as the final puff of scent left the cut glass bottle.

Mrs Hakim expected an unassuming character. Her only real reference points were the American courtroom dramas she streamed through a VPN when Aashirbaad was at work and the two younger children were off at school. Particularly fond of *The Practice*, she imagined she'd be meeting a slightly middle-aged, presumably pudgy, probably hippie, all-around geek. This was, after all, the type of person Noah attracted. That said person happened to be in the legal profession was a mystery she presumed amounted to some family connection. She read The Times and understood rich boys often end up in some alternative lifestyle or another. But opening the front door now to find a very attractive young man donning a Polo shirt, crisp chinos, and polished loafers, she took an immediate sympathy toward this last-minute guest. She wouldn't spend much time thinking how or why such a person might have become friends with her son; the important part was that he had. In the shadow of someone so obviously not Northeast London, she felt at once at ease and at a disadvantage, but a disadvantage she could not have enjoyed in anyone more brilliant or striking.

Likewise, Lilly Hakim's radiance was so paralysing, Austin found himself at once a tiny bit jealous of Noah. He remembered how his own mother had once been so beautiful, untouchable even. This led to an immediate liking for Lilly that Austin perceived could only be reciprocal.

'So, Noah tells us you're a solicitor,' she said inviting Austin through to the lounge.

'A barrister, in fact.'

'Oh goodness me,' Lilly said as she thumped Noah on the shoulder. It was only then she consciously realised the presence of her son, who evidently let himself in whilst she'd been upstairs. 'I'm afraid my son is no good with professions.' She begun to pour sweat and the little hairs around the edge of her burqa glistened as they formed into an adhesive between her scalp and the taffeta.

Austin frowned at Noah.

'Yea ... I'm uhh sorry about that, both of you.' But he didn't act sorry, and instead plopped onto the settee, leaving Austin and Lilly to face each other in an awkward juxtaposition.

Lilly smiled like a sheep and wiped a drip of perspiration from her forehead. This revelation that Austin was no ordinary lawyer raised the stakes. She felt sure she could handle the council leaders; she was a little step above them. A well-dressed middle-class white boy thrown into the mix was a different matter. For the first time in three decades, a little liquor mightn't necessarily have been a bad thing.

'So where are all the other guests?' Noah asked.

'In the dining room with your father.' She motioned across the corridor. 'I only hope he doesn't take them into the kitchen!'

'Have you prepared something special?' asked Austin, finally taking a seat next to Noah who at once scooted down to the other end of the sofa.

'Oh ... yes, that's it.' She'd have to be cleverer in her choice of words tonight. A slightly-raised hemline and Mac cosmetics would not cut it the way it did with the council.

'Well let's get to it then, eh?' said Noah. 'You go on, mum, we'll be through in a minute.'

Ordinarily this sort-of demanding behaviour from her own children would not be tolerated, but Lilly was glad for a few moments to collect herself. Making her exit from the lounge, she didn't cross the hall into the diner, but made straight for the kitchen and checked one more time that the door was properly latched.

Meanwhile, still on the settee, Austin turned to Noah. They'd not been alone since Noah texted earlier. 'Thanks for having me over to meet your family. This is unexpected and I'm really grateful.'

'Yea, listen,' Noah leaned in and lowered his voice, 'my 'rents don't know we're together, so keep it on the D.L., a'ight?'

Austin watched Noah, trying to comprehend the situation. He could *smell* the anger in his voice. He wanted to say something, to protest maybe or to make his excuses and leave, but before he had the chance, Noah got up and walked across to the dining room. Austin leaned back on the sofa, closing his eyes. He turned back to a familiar vision of kissing Noah on his soft, round, sun kissed lips. Hands pressed against his forehead, he sighed. Opening his eyes, he sat up and walked across the hallway.

Six identical dining chairs in an off-red mahogany were pushed against the walls. In the centre of the room, the table was lined down the middle with a variety of brightly-coloured dishes, most of them ceramics Lilly found on offer at the Grand Bazaar in Istanbul where she and her husband visited on their twenty-fifth anniversary. Another handful of mismatched chairs were scattered across the room. Most of these were occupied by woman dressed in long black tunics set off by bargain-basement sparkly gold or silver heels.

All the men, including Noah, were congregated near the end of the table closest to the hallway.

'Ah, Austin,' said Aashirbaad with high affectation, 'it's a pleasure to meet you. Do come through. My delightful son has told me all about you ...' — Noah glared at Austin to remind him of their 'agreement.' — '... And my wife says you're interested in Islam.'

Austin wondered how Mrs Hakim would have come up with this, but figuring it best not to ruffle feathers, he smiled. 'Yes. Culture, religion, they interest me.'

Aashirbaad proceeded to introduce Austin to each of the mosque council's members and their wives. For the second time that evening, Austin found himself correcting a member of the Hakim family for calling him a solicitor. It began to irk him, and he thought how flippant Noah was to cause this misunderstanding to begin with.

'Don't shake this one's hand,' Mr Hakim whispered in Austin's ear as they approached a woman covered head-to-toe in black. Only the slits of her eyes were visible.

'Good evening, I'm Malabika,' she said in a rehearsed manner. She rose, did a slight bow, and sat down. Austin smiled as Aashirbaad tugged him along.

'And this is Mrs Aasma Begum,' Aashirbaad said as they rounded their way to the other end of the room. 'This is a colleague of our boy Noah's, a solicitor called Austin.'

Too much wrong with this statement to correct, Austin only smiled again. He was getting good at this fake cheerfulness. 'Asthma, is it? That's an interesting name.'

'Aasma, child, A-A-S-M-A, Aasma. I'm not a disease.' The circles beneath her eyes darkened.

Austin's face reddened but Mrs Begum didn't notice.

'And yes, it is a wonderful name with an interesting meaning: "excellent." Isn't it stately?'

He worried he was meant to answer, but thankfully Lilly emerged then carrying an aluminium tray of yoghurt-based drinks. Lifting it over the heads of the ladies sat chaotically round the dining room, Austin caught a glimpse of an Ikea tag still stuck to the bottom of the tray. He took the opportunity to move to the centre of the room, anchoring himself midway between an assortment of solemn, cheaply-dressed wives at one end and giggling, gossiping men at the other.

Removing his phone from his pocket, Austin texted Zara:

-- Help! I'm in purgatory!

She wrote back:

> -- Muslims don't believe in purgatory, you twat.

Lilly continued to hand out drinks. As she neared the chair where Aasma Begum sat, a small yellow-orange cat with a long, fury tail materialised from under the table and nestled itself, unbeknownst to her, at Lilly's feet. Stepping forward with tray in hand, Lilly's black wedged espadrille stumbled over the poor cat. The tray and all its remaining contents flew through the air and landed with a whimper on Aasma's lap, splattering yoghurt on her face and chest in the process. The carroty feline dashed mid-way cross the room and sojourned herself to Austin's ankles. Had he not been so vexed, Austin might have found this whole scene funny. Only now it felt like revenge.

Mrs Begum squeaked and flailed her hands up in the air. Her husband, the council's secretary, walked over, seemingly reluctant to leave the all-male camaraderie. Noah burst into laughter and dashed off to the kitchen. At one and the same time, Lilly zipped over to her guest of honour.

'Muezza's not bothering you, is she?'

'Aren't you going to help Mrs Begum, dear?' Aashirbaad called out from amidst the men who now stopped their gossiping and stood shoulder-to-shoulder staring at the scene unfolding across the room.

'Not now,' said Lilly, matter-of-factly. Aashirbaad glared at her, not in anger, but only to detect resentment or boredom, dangerous moods that almost always led to her being sore at him.

Austin's eyes were fixed firmly on the cat, who rubbed its tail backwards and forwards across his finely-woven khaki trousers. 'Who? I thought her name is Asthma?' He said this last bit deliberately, raising his voice so the presently indisposed Mrs Begum might overhear.

'Oh, not *that* woman,' cried Lilly. 'She'll be fine.'

And she was, for Noah already returned with kitchen roll which Secretary of the Local Mosque Council Begum used to lap up tamarind-based beverage from his wife's cloak. That bits of yoghurt seeped through the fabric onto her underthings went unspoken.

'Muezza is the cat,' Lilly said.

This was the perfect segue, thought Aashirbaad whose attention fluxed between the Begums and his own wife, eager to latch onto whichever position proved the more lucrative. With a broad smile fixed on his face, he patted the council president on the back to say, 'I've got this,' and hopped from step to step, a lion snatching at its prey.

'According to Islamic tradition, Muezza was the prophet Muhammad's favourite cat — peace be upon him,' he said approaching Austin.

Austin looked plaintively at Lilly, a wordless sympathy mounted between them. How long Aashirbaad had been standing there or where he'd come from was either of their guesses.

'Peace be upon whom, dear?' said Lilly, fixing her hold on Austin but signifying with the tilt of her head to her husband. 'Muhammad or the cat?'

All the women found this inordinately hilarious. Even Malabika, who had been silent all evening, now raised her niqab, revealing a long smile and beautiful eyelashes. Lilly saw this and her own face went sour sensing competition. Malabika was not the scared kitten the party's hostess wanted her to be.

Aashirbaad turned to his wife but addressed the entire female delegation. 'You may think it is funny, but a cat is the quintessential pet.' The Hakims had a special ability to use two senses at the same time: looking at one person whilst speaking to another.

'Oh, come now, we're but making light.' She let go of Austin's eyes and transfixed her gaze on her husband, grabbing him affectionately under the arm. 'It wouldn't hurt *you* to lighten up.'

In such situations, Austin always trusted it to be his obligation, nay duty, to soothe things over. Confrontation made him uncomfortable, which was rather ironic for someone with a legal background. Whether his particular conviction came out of his profession or from some moral quandary was irrelevant then. He witnessed the entire conversation but was still uncertain of its aims, if conversations could be said to have aims for themselves.

'What was it you were saying about the cat, Mr Hakim?'

'Yes, dear, do go on,' Lilly said, reinforcing her grip under her husband's scrawny bicep.

Aashirbaad's face pulsed with pleasure. 'Well, you see,' he turned with Lilly still in tow to face the entire room, 'Muhammad, peace be upon *him*, awoke one day to the sounds of the adhan — that's the call to prayer for our non-Muslim friends in the room.'

Austin felt sheepish and glanced over at Noah for reassurance, but Noah left the room.

Mr Hakim continued talking: 'Preparing to attend prayer, Muhammad began to dress. He soon discovered, however, that his cat was sleeping on the sleeve of his prayer robe. Rather than wake tiny Muezza, he used a pair of scissors to cut the sleeve off and left the cat undisturbed. Isn't that brilliant!'

Everyone, including Aasma Begum, giggled on cue. Peace was restored. Austin grew self-righteous; this was his doing.

Meanwhile, Aashirbaad himself felt quite smug. 'Come, let us eat.'

Plates were passed and all envoys to the Hakim Eid celebration took their turns at the makeshift buffet. Seating arrangements still remained rather dubious and again Austin found himself lodged between the sexes who recongregated into their respective groups. On the plus side, he was thankful Malabika had now fully taken her face veil off; he began earlier to worry how she might eat if it remained on. Lilly, on the other hand, would have rather seen Malabika starve than absorb any of her own spotlight. In-between bites of a layered paratha with an eggy coating, Austin caught Noah's eye. At some point between his father's cat story and the start of dinner, Noah returned to the dining room. Austin was glad to see him approach.

The eldest Hakim boy carried a dubious look. His deep-set eyes were red, and his pupils froze in dilation. 'Everything cool?' he said, 'It's been a bit awkward and all.'

'Not at all.' Austin did his best to morph his face into party-mode. 'Anyhow, thank you again for the invitation. It's been an interesting evening, to say the least.'

'Well thank you so much for coming.'

This sounded so disingenuous that Austin took a moment to think over his next line.

'I'm simply privileged to have been invited. What a wonderful celebration, like Christmas really. I suppose that must be how it is for you. It must be like the biggest holiday of the year.'

Noah knew he hadn't said any of this to Austin, but he was grateful it had been sensed. In fact, despite the intrusion of the local mosque council and despite his father's attempt to quell the festive spirit, it had been *felt*.

'It is such a nice thing,' he said, and then noticing the cat again at Austin's feet, he added: 'Should I do something about her?'

'Oh no, leave Muezza alone. I think she's about as wonderful as your mother.'

A calm settled on Noah. 'Let's go back to yours tonight, eh?'

The sun shining through the window of the tiny bedroom in St Johns Wood refracted into a dozen shades of yellow and orange splayed across the visible slithers of hardwood floors. The room was large enough for nothing more than Austin's double bed and a side table, but looking out through the window, he could almost picture the spires of Prague's old town, a place he visited years ago on holiday. Thin, splintering Gothic towers of sandstone and iron. Delicate rococo façades. It was a mirage, of course. In actuality, his bedroom looked out on Abbey Road Studios. Not a bad view, if you're into a particular brand of Liverpudlian music (he was, alas, not), but definitely not the cobbled streets of the Czech capital. But he was in a romantic mood this morning, on account of waking up to Noah snuggled into his right body cavity.

'Got any coffee?' Noah said as he rolled over, his hairy chest bare and his lower-half covered with nothing but the bedsheet.

Austin waved in the direction of the kitchen. He watched as Noah got up and walked to the other side of the flat, his member flopping freely the whole way. His confidence in his own body, or his lack of shame thereof, astounded Austin who was even too self-conscious to go to the loo in the middle of the night without first slipping on boxer shorts.

'I guessed you take milk and sugar,' Noah said, handing Austin a mug.

'No, black, just black,' he said, taking it anyway.

Noah sat back down on the edge of the bed. 'Well don't look so shocked, eh! You've seen a dick before.'

Austin wanted to say that yes, of course, he had. But never one so beautiful, never one that made love to him in the way Noah had last night. Never one so brazenly gorgeous at eight-thirty on a Sunday. Surrounded by the morning sun, Austin saw that the upper bit of Noah's bronzed legs were dotted with small scars. These were pinkish and brown and almost looked like the ends of a cigarette had been put out on his skin. An image of his client Olivia floated to the forefront of his mind. He could remember the ends of Olivia's fingers having those very same amaranth pink stubs of scar.

'I enjoyed last night,' Austin said, shifting his brain to more pleasant thoughts.

'Yea, it was cool.' Noah's eyes darted. He shifted a bit in the bed and pulled the sheet over his crotch. 'I reconnected with this chick a few days back, yea? She was a right looker —' Noah's accent changed, became more street. Austin looked through Noah, fixing his attention on a mark on the wall beyond the outline of his forehead. '— She was so tight in all the right places, you feel me?'

Austin felt something on his shoulder and looked up to find Noah shaking him.

'Said, do you feel me?'

It took Austin a moment to process what this meant. 'Do you mean you're bisexual or something?'

'I told you I don't do labels.'

Austin tried to connect the dots. Noah had always been cagey with calling himself gay, and there was the odd thing of his being invited to the family house but only as a 'friend,' and of course the periods of silence occurring more and more regularly. 'I just want to know if this is something real ... I mean, why are you telling me about this girl you slept with?'

'Well anyway, don't matter,' said Noah now. 'She was this good Muslim girl, that's all I'm saying.'

'What's that got to do with anything?'

'Just if my family found out I was with a kaafir, they would probably kill me. I mean, a man is okay, but a non-Muslim one ... shiitttt.'

In fact, neither Lilly nor Aashirbaad gave Noah any indication they would be fine with him dating a man. In the aftermath of the Hakim Eid celebration, Mr Hakim resumed making mental plans for his son's eventual marriage to Tiara Rose ('I still want to get to know that young lady,' he proclaimed on learning she couldn't attend) and Mrs Hakim, well, she fancied Austin more for herself.

'I can't convert after two coffee dates and one night of passion,' Austin said half as a joke, but more concerned with what hid in the recesses of Noah's mind.

Noah put on the crumpled jeans he'd thrown across the room the night before. The comment was lost on him, as he still rambled on about the girl. 'Islam means "voluntary submission to God." All I got to say is she submitted to me that night.' Noah chuckled.

Changing the subject, Austin asked Noah what he'd like to do in the afternoon. In Austin's book, this was a given. Rule no. 4: If someone stays over, you entertain him the next day. There were no one-night stands. Not since Antonio.

Noah took down his t-shirt from a hook on the back of the bedroom door. He reached in the front pocket and pulled out a reflector band of the type a bicyclist wears. 'Actually, I got to go. But don't worry, I'll be back again sometime.'

'No problem,' said Austin, though it was a huge problem when one of the rules were broken.

Noah was already out on the pavement putting on his helmet when Austin picked up his mobile phone.

'Hello, mum? ... It's me, Austin ... I think I've got myself into some trouble ... I'm inside my head over this guy ...'

'You don't need anyone else, son ... You are strong ... You've got this!'

Her voice enough, Austin dissolved into tears.

Where did it begin? Noah couldn't remember now. It seemed to have always been here, although that couldn't be true. He could recall a time, maybe a decade ago, maybe less, when it wasn't necessary. But even then, it had been there, he considered, not in an addictive way: in those days it still felt like fun.

All of this rushed through his brain as he sat on the toilet at New Bloomsbury Set, a basement bar near Russell Square station, and took a swig of the Miller High Life he brought in the loo with him. The noise and stench of the tiny barroom could still be heard and smelt from the bathroom stall. He'd come here to hide out, to have two or three minutes to himself before heading back out to the ruckus of his colleagues from the Midwifery Council. It was a monthly ritual, their going-out to a bar selected in turns by each of the clerks.

Bloomsbury was situated as about far west as he allowed himself to go and the beer helped balanced the pressure.

Imagine having the life you always imagined having. So read the sticker pasted onto the back of the toilet door. Trouble was, he couldn't imagine any other miserable life than the one he was living right now. It might all be clearer if he could have a bump right now. Then again, maybe not. A small voice shouted from somewhere behind the toilet cubicle, its source his own submerged conscience, warning him this epidemic lack of clarity might be *because* of the coke. This voice was one of the many he'd been hearing lately. Most were hungry voices needing to be fed.

He stepped outside the stall and looked into the opaque mirror hung over a flimsy-looking stainless-steel sink. A tribal warrior ogled back in the reflection. He wore a long piece of buckskin over loose-fitting deerskin leggings. The buckskin had been brought through the centre of the legs and looped over and under a calfskin belt. He recognised it, a Comanche. He knew the Comanche. He always made an appearance when Noah became vulnerable.

He scrubbed his hands and splashed water onto his face. The Comanche warrior disappeared, and Noah saw himself as he was: ragged with deep-set circles under his eyes. He needed sleep. He wanted another Miller.

Asha waited there for him to step out of the loo.

'Come in here,' she said, motioning to the women's room.

A tattoo had been grazed onto the right side of her neck. For some reason, Noah had never seen it before. They worked three desks away from each other, but this was the first time he noticed. Maybe she covers it up, he thought. It looked like a shuffled deck of cards; the Ace of Spades on top.

'I could use some luck tonight,' he said, motioning at her jugular as they walked through the door with a W on it.

'I'm chuffed you like it, yea ... The spade represents a thief.'

'What do you steal?'

'Hearts, mostly.'

This kind of girl is the problem for you. That same small voice followed him in here. Her type has always been the problem, he knew this. The exotic girls, the party animals, the good-girls-gone-bad. Every single bad straight porn video he ever saw rolled up into one and presenting itself as a Punjabi sister with hair both as straight and as dark as you'd ever see.

She pulled him by the shirt, revealing a pint-size of skin between his naval and boxer shorts, which she ran her long, pink-painted fingernails over. As he moved to kiss her, she pushed him into one of the two stalls in this tiny bathroom. On the toilet seat, she prepared two thin white lines.

'Hit?' she asked.

'Word,' he said as he squatted down on both knees.

With 19,607 bus stops in contrast to 270 tube stations, there are some parts of London reachable only by double decker. Austin got up early in order to pay a call to one such part, near the Willowbrook Estate in the southeast. By seven, he had showered, dressed, and was out the door with keys in his right pocket and his briefcase sashaying in his left hand. He observed himself in mirrors of the lift on the ride down to the ground floor. He wanted to look lawyerly but not cocky. The trick was to balance a sense of street smarts with a look of authority so you didn't get messed about with. Had Austin done his research, or read the brief his clerk prepared, he might have known Willowbrook was largely and comprehensively refurbished a few years back, and even prior to that had always been an untroubled low-rise estate of four-storey maisonette blocks. It was not the behemoth housing project of his imagination where drug lords roam free and prostitutes are available for a tuppence.

According to Google maps, he could take the Jubilee line and connect to the bus. Forty-five minutes if traffic cooperated. The first order of business, though, was coffee. There was a small coffee shop next to the station. It was the kind of place that cannot properly be called a shop, for it was more a kiosk with one solid back wall and two sort-of half side walls and a long low counter separating a single barista from a throng of TfL passengers that had all, like Austin, been in too much of a rush to go to Starbucks or Paul or Costa. Despite its looks, then, this coffee shop did quite well as it offered certain constants: coffee (labelled fair trade but really just bad) and an attractive barista (really just the ripped nephew of the rabbi up the road). Austin had been here hundreds, maybe thousands, of times. Always the same bad coffee, always the same boy. He didn't wear a name tag and so far as Austin was concerned, didn't have or need a name. He was the barista who would eye fuck anyone. He'd make eye contact with you after you ordered your filter coffee (really just

Nescafe) and hold it for three-to-five seconds, making you think of all the dirty things you want to do to him. If he had a name-tag it only would have the initials DTEF. Down to eye fuck.

'That will be two quid,' DTEF said, handing over the paper-based cup.

Austin passed over a two-pound coin. The barista fixed his gaze. One-one-thousand, two-one-thousand, three-one-thousand.

'Have a nice day, mate.'

Sometimes people gave the barista a tip, Austin saw them do it. But he never had. For one thing, two pounds for instant coffee was rich, and furthermore he didn't feel right doing it, being neither Jewish nor the type to pay for sex of any variety.

Eleven minutes later he was in Southwark. A bus approached. Austin was still nursing his coffee and didn't pay attention to the number. It was only when he sat down that he realised he made a mistake and instead of connecting to the 63 ended up on the 136. It was going in the same direction, though, more-or-less.

The number 136 is most alliterative bus route in London; it has eight stops beginning with L in sequential order. And so it began: Lewisham Hospital (several elderly and sick-looking folks got on), Lewisham Park (a lady with her French bull-dog), Lewisham Fire Station (nothing), Lewisham Centre (endless streams of bags from Debenhams), Lewisham Clock Tower (pretty), Lewisham Station (connects to the DLR), Loampit Vale / Jerrard Street (relief it doesn't start with Lewisham). By the time he at last alighted at East Street, Austin grew restless, was ten minutes behind schedule, and still needed to walk another mile to the housing estate.

Twenty-three minutes and four major crosswalks later, Austin arrived at the main gates of the Willowbrook Estate. The parking lots were busy, much busier than his own neighbourhood at this time of morning. How strange it was to see everyone in baker's smocks, nurse's scrubs, fast food chain-issued uniforms. And yet they all hurried past him as though he were a local. No one looked twice. It seemed to be a place where everyone was welcome and thus everybody was ignored.

The doorways at each maisonette had multiple bells for the flats above. Austin checked the brief. Apartment 3B. Etta Daniels, fifty-six years old, disabled.

'Hello, Ms Daniels?'

Someone was there; the intercom came on. But now silence.

'Etta Daniels? It's Austin, I'm your barrister ...'

'The *barrister*?' Ms Daniels was half-awake; her sleepy South London accent was rough and full of question. 'What are you doing *here*?'

It started to rain a little now and Austin moved under the awning, straining his neck so his voice could still be heard over the intercom. 'We have an appointment?'

Silence again.

'Your solicitor, he said he notified you —'

'Why for?' She sounded more awake now, like her brain suddenly switched on.

'— that I would be coming to visit to discuss your case.'

Austin released the intercom and tried to pull himself further underneath the plastic awning. It began to rain harder and his mohair suit trickled with the wet. It had the habit of smelling downright awful when even a little damp.

He heard the intercom click on again and then something like a shout coming from the speaker.

'Why did you come here!'

He grew frustrated now. It was well past the time of their appointment and whatever mistrust Etta Daniels had in visitors seemed out of place for a woman accused of public intoxication and possession of cannabis, a woman who needed legal representation.

'Look,' shouted Austin in the direction of the intercom, 'I'm paying you a call to *help* you —'

'... It weren't like it was an accident ...' She spoke to someone else now, her voice further away from the intercom.

'— So, are you going to let me in or what?'

'No.'

Right then. He ran the three minutes through the rain to the correct bus stop and did the whole journey home all over again.

After bunking down for the better part of the afternoon, throwing himself into the countless emails piling up on the laptop sat on a tiny big-box-store-desk cum makeshift home office, Austin had a phone call.

'Any news, bruh?' the voice asked from the end of the other line.

'Bruh? ... What?! ... Noah?'

'Yea, it's me. Calling to check on you. Been wondering why you haven't been in touch, like a text or something. I thought we were getting on real well.'

The truth was Austin wanted to get in touch with Noah. He had, in fact, picked up his mobile several times intending to do that. But never quite knowing what to say, he would instead decide to send a text. But then not knowing what to type, he would abandon the phone altogether. After going through this routine so many times, he resolved to wait for Noah to get in touch with him this time. When that didn't happen, Austin chalked it up to that old phrase which so many use as an excuse for not making the next move — *The line works both ways.*

'I've been thinking a lot about you,' he settled on.

'Yea, I've been thinking about you too.' — Austin sprang from his seat and began pacing the room. — 'In fact, I thought maybe I scared you off with that stuff about fucking the Muslim girl.'

Austin sat back down. Never a fan of using phrases like 'fuck' or 'shag' instead of something more couth such as 'make love,' he winced. Rule No. 5: Don't curse if a non-expletive will do just as well. (He regularly broke this rule, but like most of the rules, they applied more to other people than to Austin himself.)

'No, it's cool,' he lied.

'You wanna go out tonight? Dinner?'

After putting on his jeans and sneakers, Noah walked over to the small bookshelf in the corner of his studio flat. He picked up the novel that broke his heart a decade ago. Those were the days when he could still find the energy to read. He was always lethargic now, and he'd sit and stare into space for hours that would feel like minutes, waiting for someone to call, waiting for the next hit. He wanted to hold the weight of the book's paper and to connect with its sorrow. As he opened it, he found a shiny, dark strand of his hair caught between the pages. He wondered if pieces of his former self were left in all of the books he read, or if perhaps they'd left pieces in him. It wasn't for lack of trying. He wanted Austin to be the one to take him away from his miserable existence. Take away, but also join. Confusing, wasn't it, what he wanted. So much so he resolved then, flipping through the old novel's pages, to take it one day at a time. This would be easier, he thought; it was how he approached everything else.

Haquenée is the French word used to describe a small breed of horse. Looking up and down Richmond Road, Noah could almost imagine high-stepping horses and horse-drawn carriages where bearded white hipsters and man-bun-wearing Asians now roamed the streets. These were the things he loved about the Hackney area of London: beer in familiar bottles and a short but sweet cocktail list (ideal for someone that only started drinking at age twenty-five, post-mosque going), substantial burgers with wholegrain buns and no real websites to describe what's on (instead, check the blogs). So unlike the mediocrity of Mayfair or Soho. And, for the same reasons, these were also all the things Austin hated about not just Hackney, but about East London in general.

They settled on LARDON — stylised this way in all capital letters — on account that Noah heard, ironically given the restaurant's undoubted connection with pork, that this was *the best Italian in all of London.*

Reproductions of paintings of Old Rome lined the walls interspersed with autographed photographs of YouTube and podcast celebrities who'd eaten at one of the restaurant's eleven tables. The tiny gaps between picture frames were all that was visible of the off-colour white plasterboard as though the decorator thought there is nothing worse than staring at a bare wall. Noah and Austin sat at table two, designated by the number 2 carved into the plywood table top. The large window opposite framed a view of the London Fields, a former animal grazing land turned open-air park.

'There are so many elements you have to take into mind,' Noah said as they sat. 'The design, the lighting, the energy — that's a big one.' He said all this as if he were an interior designer or restaurant critic. 'You need a focal point so the conversation can ebb and flow.'

Austin nodded his head in agreement, no idea what Noah was on about. 'So how have you been?' he said, changing the subject.

'Been working and thinking a lot. Trying to think what to do about my sister ...'

The menus arrived then, delivered by a waiter with *indie* embroidered on his t-shirt. Of course, thought Austin.

'Oh? I didn't know you had other siblings.'

'Just one, besides the boys. My sister, she's eighteen. When my parents split up temporarily last year, she came to live with me and now she's going off to uni. Up north somewhere. Leicester, I think she said.' This was all news to Austin, who wondered what caused the change in Noah to have turned him into someone willing to share elements of his personal life so freely.

'And you're worried she won't be able to cope?'

'Nah, she'll be fine. She's smart and all. But she needs to get a job, make some money up there in the Midlands. I can't support her; she's got to take loans as it is.'

'What about your parents?'

Noah winced. 'They got too much on their plate.'

Austin was not blind to the class differences between himself and the Hakims, but Lilly and Aashirbaad did not strike him as the kind of parents that wouldn't look after their children. He waved to the waiter, not sure what to say.

'I dropped outta school myself,' Noah said now. More news to Austin, who found this bit of information troubling. 'I couldn't cope with the pressure. You're supposed to be bloody perfect when there's so much temptation around.'

Having believed neither of those things with any particular strength, Austin nodded his head again.

'Anyway, I said to my sister she can get a job at a place like this. Be a waitress or bus tables or something.'

'But not a place like *this*,' Austin said.

'I dunno why you care where she works. But I get it, this is not your kind of joint.'

'It's trying too hard.' His eyes scanned the endless frames lining the walls. 'And so are the people. Did you see our waiter's top? Everybody is trying so damn hard to be alternative, to be "indie" or whatever; they lose their identities. When everyone tries uniqueness in the same way, they all end up being the same.'

'I said I get it. Not your kind of place.'

Austin couldn't give up making his point. 'It's not just this place, though. It's the whole scene. It feels like an attack on middle class values. On my values, in fact. The ones I grew up with. All these East Londoners and now even some South Londoners and Brooklynites and I don't-know-who-else all parading around against consumerism and pop culture and conformity when, in fact the ease at which their own subculture can be appropriated, repackaged, and marketed back to them makes them the ultimate conformists.'

Austin at his ripest, Noah thought. Like an apple sitting around too long that begins to get mushy. 'It's cool you have opinions, but I really just wanted to talk about my sister getting a job. And anyway, I can't figure out why you care where.'

'Yes, well, I care because it's your sister, and I care for you.'

They sat in silence for some moments, until the indie waiter came round to take their orders. Noah ordered a simple spaghetti with parmesan, finding it hard to choose anything on the menu that didn't include pork. Told you so, thought Austin. Hipsters love bacon.

'It seems to me everything's changed,' Austin said now to try to put himself into better standing.

'"Jack of all trades, master of none" is the phrase I remember hearing a lot as a kid. I was exposed to a load of different things growing up — activities, sports, languages, exotic travel, and different kinds of people. My family wanted me to have as many first-hand experiences as possible, so I could make up my own mind about something or someone.'

Austin ran his fingers through his hair, which, unlike Noah's balding scalp, was a full head of brown locks.

'I just can't tell you how everything's changed now that everybody wants to be the same.'

'You sound so fucking old, mate.'

Austin nodded. It wasn't that he was unsympathetic to people in their twenties, he envied them. Those ten years in his life had been a growth-spurt driven, habit-forming decade. Never again, he thought, would he experience the time and space to explore new things through the lens of self-discovery. Now he was amidst the decade of earn your keep. His whole life now seemed to be driven by work, money, and the search for something meaningful. What he saw in this restaurant, in the waiter, and indeed in Noah was a freedom he either no longer possessed or never wanted to begin with.

'Anyway, it's really good to see you, Noah.'

'You too. You look different though.' Austin's skin was pasty, and he seemed to have gotten thinner and frailer since Noah stayed over.

'I've been working quite a lot, so I'm tired.' Austin was embarrassed he hadn't put more effort in, at least changed shirts or sprayed some cologne, but he'd taken the tube to Hackney straight from the office. 'I was also a bit ill for a few days after we saw each other last.'

'Did my mum scare you off?' Noah quipped.

Austin gave an awkward smile.

'I mean ... Is everything cool now?'

'Yea fit as a fiddle now. It was a stomach flu, I think, like being bulimic without a choice.' The food arrived just then, and Austin again felt awkward at his word choice.

'So long as you're fine.' Noah looked down at his plate of spaghetti. 'I'm always afraid when the order of the next table over is delivered, I'll be envious.'

'Oh yea, I can appreciate what you mean,' said Austin. 'And I never even saw what they're having listed on the menu.'

'I think we're safe this time.' He twisted a strand of pasta around his fork. 'The Italians say the water you cook pasta in should be as salty as the Mediterranean.'

Austin could relate. He was like somebody who contains large quantities of sodium chloride, thus causing him to be salty. But he couldn't place his finger on why. Everything about Noah looked right and he often, Austin had to admit, said the right things. But in these moments, when his words were flat, and his speech clipped, Austin thought he could sense something dark in Noah, someone who was only superficially interested in other people. In this way, Noah was like a mirror to Austin's own insecurities. It was in these moments Austin knew, intellectually, what it means to see yourself reflected back at you, that there is no room for blame, there is no room for judgement, and there is no room to feel like a victim of another person's actions or words. There is only room for real love based on understanding and gratitude. He knew this all intellectually, but not emotionally. Mirror mirror on the wall, who's the most broken of them all?

After dessert, they walked through Shacklewell Lane, a multicultural melt of young parents, misfits, and street artists wedged between Dalston and Hackney. Noah considered himself a card-carrying member of the second set. The official easy-going vibe did it for him, as did the hummus served at every third cafe, and the lack of any chain restaurants save the singular Nando's. He brought Austin here for a reason.

'East Londoners are the only people in the world,' he said, 'who can cohabitate and not kill each other in the process. That thing you said earlier about being a jack of all trades? For me, that's what this road is all about: the multiculturalism. Loads of different identities are here.' He pointed to the storefronts lining Shacklewell Lane. 'Look, you see shops owned by Greek people, Turks, Caribbean people, Africans from every part of the continent. All on this one road. It's like in its own way teaching us how to get along.'

Austin agreed, but for reasons closer to home. A memory of visiting Athens as a child came into this head. His grandmother had taken him there to see the Acropolis and the Parthenon. He spent weeks reading Herodotus' history of Ancient Greece before their trip, no small feat for a fourteen-year old boy. On the last day there, his nan took him to a traditional taverna, filled with people of all complexions and all speaking in tongues he'd never heard before. He could still smell the filo pastry. Though he wouldn't mention it aloud, it was one of his few happy childhood memories.

But no matter how hard he tried, Austin couldn't see his values personified in anything about this place that was so special to Noah.

Though the mirror incarnate in Noah grew in clarity, Austin could never be inside Noah's head. This bothered him immensely. The guard dogs of Noah's mind were rabid, they were the watchmen on the wall aiming their guns should anyone get too close.

'Let's go back to yours,' Noah said, when they came to the end of the high road.

'Oh, okay.' Austin didn't expect to be offered this after his less than enthusiastic behaviour.

So they spent that night together at Austin's place, even though Noah's was closer.

Noah Hakim took hostages wherever he went. Not physical ones, emotional hostages. Last night he texted Asha. For no reason. Or maybe to score some coke. Either way, it didn't work out. Then he got on Facebook to check on Tiara Rose. Why had she ghosted him? Oh, he remembered now, he had been the one to ignore her. Tonight, he sat staring out the window, doing nothing except hitting the screen of his iPhone 3G in intervals of twenty to thirty seconds to get the backlight to pop on. The flash of bright white made him come alive, a temporary reprieve from the numbness of the sedative effects of this provisional sobriety. He did not know what to do with himself, waiting for a feeling. But it had been so long since he'd had an honest-to-Allah emotion that wasn't under the supervision of a chemical agent that he wasn't even sure he'd recognise it when it arrives.

This is bollocks. Pulling on a pair of beat-up Converse, he rolled himself off the sofa and flung his mobile phone into the pocket of his sweatpants. Walking down the high road used to mean something. The colours, the sounds, the smells. They were all their own stimulants for anyone without means to the drugs that cost paper. It was never as good as the euphoria from using, but it had been something, some kind of distraction. It felt so empty now. He stopped into an off-license and picked up a Tall Boy disguised not-so-cleverly in a brown paper bag. The can was empty within a quarter of an hour. He walked past one of those special bins put out by the council for disposing of dog doo and dropped the empty beer can in.

'Hey! What do you think yer doin'?' came a shrill Cockney cry from behind.

Noah didn't bother to turn around. 'Uh, I'm putting something in the bin. Right.'

'Tryin' to get into Barney Rubble? That there bin is for pet waste only.'

Noah turned around, a little alcohol had no effect on him. Rhyming slang had never been his thing, but hey this was better than sitting idly at home. He looked down at the receptacle, there were two other cans of 4.2% Guinness and at least one can of 5.4% Blue Moon that he could see. His tongue began to loosen a little.

'Looks like a normal arse bin to me.'

The voice belonged to a gruffy looking man with thick eyebrows who came nearer now and pointed to a tin-metal sign attached to a pole.

'Says right there: Dog Shit Only.'

Now to be fair, the sign said something rather politer. There was something so self-disciplined about it. Noah didn't give two fucks about the dark life of some council-paid worker whose only job was to go around collecting the rubbish from these bins.

'Well I'll be brown bread,' he said using the only rhyming slang he could remember. 'Wouldn't you know it. I wouldn't wanna contaminate all that lovely clean animal faeces with a bloody beer can, would I?'

He had a look of such seriousness on his face that it could have scared even the worst street gang member into submission. The face was no match for a scruffy East-Ender. The man soon scurried off. Noah felt like David slaying Goliath with one fell swoop.

Just then the phone in his pocket buzzed. I'm gonna get my fix after all, he thought, but then his temporary joy turned to mild disappointment to see it was Austin texting.

-- Hello Noah, would you like to go for dinner tomorrow night? X

-- Yo, perfect timing.

-- I've made a reservation in Mayfair. I'll send over the details.

For fuck's sake. This was revenge for LARDON.

Austin stared at the hostess. 'Could you check again?'

The restaurant hostess (Were they still called that, or did they have posher names now like airline stewardesses baptised flight attendants? Or was it cabin crew?) gave him a long, low look, her skinny eyebrows sticking out over her glasses. 'I've checked twice already.' She had that particular British candour he found insufferable. It was more than her words, it was her whole look.

'Yes, well, check again?' — Her waist length hair was putting him off; it needed to be tied back. — 'He was supposed to be here at eight o'clock.'

It was 08:21 and Austin had spent those twenty-one minutes (technically twenty-six, since he made it a rule to arrive everywhere five minutes early) pacing up and down the entryway, checking the main door, popping his head outside, asking the receptionist, rinse and repeat.

At 08:25, he began to make his way to the door in a final act of a dramatic *au revoir* when the receptionist flagged him down. 'Sorry, sir! ... Yes, you, sir ... Mr Hakim just arrived at the side entrance —'

'Oh okay ...' Austin hadn't realised there was a side entrance or otherwise he would have been checking it too.

'— He's being seated now.'

'If you feel a connection, don't be shy about it, yea?'

'Sorry?' Austin failed to hear the last three or four sentences, maybe paragraphs, Noah said. He knifed at his tilapia, flaking away little bits. 'Sorry, I missed that.'

Noah propelled his cloth napkin onto the table. 'You still pissed at me?'

'Do you realise what sort of place we're in? Do you realise how many strings I pulled to get us a table on a Saturday night? Do you ....' His voice trailed off on noticing the buttery lard stains on the napkin. That's what napkins are for — wiping one's face and hands, especially useful when one eats lobster — but they ought to stay white.

'I told you. I was dealing with some personal stuff. My sister, yea?'

In that moment, Noah looked so disappointed in himself, so close to tears in fact, that Austin could do nothing but flake another bit away from his fish and smile sympathetically.

'I'm sorry,' he said, with only a slight passing thought as to why he should be the one apologising.

'No worries.' Noah grinned, his almost-tears almost instantly drying. 'I am just sayin' if you have feelings for me, don't hide them.'

Against his better breeding, this almost made Austin laugh aloud. 'I thought I've been perfectly clear that I feel for you.'

Noah placed the yellowing napkin back on his lap and reached for the stainless-steel lobster pick. 'Just don't be shy.'

Though it irritated him to play word games, Austin began to follow into this bottomless abyss. 'What's an example of not being shy?'

No response. Scooping out meat from inside the lobster seemed more of a priority at the moment.

'Inviting you on this date wasn't shy, was it?'

Noah neatly positioned the protracted cylindrical handle ending in a crescent-shaped pick next to his wine glass. 'Suppose it wasn't.'

'But there is something I want to give you.' Austin reached for the inside pocket of his Sandro blazer.

'Aww shucks, mister, you shouldn't have,' Noah said with such a lame American accent that Austin paused pulling out the small envelope from the pocket. Noah could see that the joke hadn't landed well, so made to correct himself and put on his best posh accent, typically reserved for holy men and government officials. He realised long ago that with this manner of speaking whatever he happened to be talking about had a greater chance of being taken seriously. 'It's sweet of you to think of me, darling.'

At hearing this, Austin's hand flew so quickly out of the blazer pocket that the small flower-card-sized envelope tumbled onto his plate and into a mound of flaked tilapia.

Noah let out a gleeful chuckle as he reached across the table for the envelope, picking it out of the fish as though his own fingers were a fork. Austin could taste bubbles travel up along his spine almost to the top of his throat. The panic prickled a bit. Not knowing what else to do, he began talking as if nothing peculiar was going on.

Inside, he recoiled with disgrace and apprehension.

'It's a key,' Austin said as Noah opened the envelope, 'to my flat.'

Their eyes bored into one another, the receiver's in a look of consternation and the giver's with an air of trepidation. 'Just in case you want to stay over more frequently, let yourself in after work, that sort of thing.'

'So, it's not an offer to move in ...,' Noah said. Thank Fuck is what he thought.

Austin couldn't tell if this was disappointment or defeat speaking. 'One thing at a time, no?'

'Yes. One thing at a time.'

Saturday mornings were Austin's favourite time of the week. The dawn of a fresh weekend, two whole days of doing whatever one wanted before the rat race commenced again on Monday. To his pleasant surprise, Noah was using his key with regularity. Friday nights into Saturday mornings now had an even greater meaning waking up to the sounds of Noah's humble snore. This morning, though, he awoke to a draft of cold air, a heavy bass line, and a rhythmic beatboxing all originating in the direction of the living room.

'What the hell is that?' Austin screamed over the hip-hop playing from YouTube.

Noah sat cross-legged on the floor with an assortment of white papers and tiny plastic bags surrounding him.

'Chill out, geez, it's to help me relax.' Noah licked the end of a blunt and pressed the papers together. 'You might try some.'

Austin yanked the blunt out of his houseguest's hand. 'You can't do that shit in my house.'

'So, you don't care if I do it, you just don't want me to do it here?' He gave a little laugh. 'Okay then.'

Austin threw the blunt out the balcony doors and then slammed them shut. 'You think you're clever?'

Noah shrugged and took out another piece of thin paper from its cardboard case.

'Can you imagine how many people I've seen go down on drug charges? Do you forget what kind of lawyer I am? Are you some kind of idiot?'

None of these questions demanded a response, and yet Noah felt obliged to give one.

'It's just my thing, yo. Like you've got your classical music and theatre and all. I've got this. Rap and weed; they like go together.'

'Not in my flat they don't. And why are you speaking like this?'

Noah was getting right tired of people trying to tell him what sort of words he should use and how he should sound. He clutched onto the nauseousness in the back of his mouth and began gathering up his stuff.

'Right then, I'm out yo.'

With Noah gone, Austin sat on the sofa in disbelief. You think you know someone, he thought to himself, but then couldn't think of how to end the phrase. After some minutes, he realised the YouTube channel still played from his Smart TV. Searching for the remote on the coffee table, he saw a small white envelope, of the kind a gift card might come in. It had to be Noah's, his bad habit of leaving things wherever he went. Inside the envelope was a fine white powder. Austin wasn't street-wise, nor would he have ever professed to be, but he knew someone who was.

Taking out his phone, he snapped a picture of the envelope's contents and sent it to Zara.

-- I'm sorry, A., but looks like snow to me.

-- Snow? Zara be serious.

-- I am ... Snow. It's another name for cocaine. My god you're so white.

Jesus. Is this what Noah's into? He needed to be sure. He opened WhatsApp.

-- Noah, look forget about the weed. It's not a big deal.

It was, in fact, but he had more important things to consider now.

-- OK, thanks babe. I gotta do my own thing this afternoon anyway. Call you later.

-- Wait, before you go ... I found this packet on the table.

Austin attached the image. It took ninety-two seconds for Noah to respond.

-- Oh, that's sugar. You know I like sugar in my tea and you don't have any so I brought it along. You can keep it there for next time I'm round.

-- Okay. Xx

Austin picked up the remote and switched off the television. It had been wrong to freak out, he thought, and he began chastising himself for the lack of trust in Noah. The weed wasn't okay, but everyone has a vice, that much is true.

Later that afternoon, Austin put on the filter coffee machine to brew. As the liquid began to percolate, he opened the kitchen cabinet to take down a mug. There on the second shelf stood a blue and white container of Tate & Lyle Sugar.

What do you do when you find out that someone you love is using?

Confront Noah about it. If he loves me, he'll quit. That's logical. But no, that won't work. Enough of his clients used for him to know that the compulsion to get more drugs is bigger than the person, and usually it's bigger than his love for other people. Maybe rehab, or an intervention? He could ask Zara to help. But addicts can be very unpredictable in their words and behaviour, Noah didn't seem all that unpredictable, no more so than Austin himself. Fuck! He stared at his phone. What's your next move, man?

But some people are just curious, right? They try drugs once or twice to see what it's like and then decide to leave it. Yes, that had to be it. Most people who try drugs don't continue using them. He'll leave it then. Best to leave it. And if he sees it again then, yes, maybe then he'll say something.

What do you do when someone finds out you're using?

So stupid to just leave stuff laying around. But perhaps he wanted to get caught. It added to the excitement of the game, or maybe he wanted to ask for help, like subconsciously or something. Austin's not that daft, right? He must have known what it is. But then again, he's not exactly street-wise. He might even think it's taboo to bring it up.

But just play it cool, right? The butter-wouldn't-melt facial expression and tone of voice will convince him, it's worked on everybody else, for what ten years now? It will work at least long enough to give him the benefit of the doubt; it's him who is in the wrong for not trusting you.

Mid-December rolled around. As other people were busy closing in on their families — shopping for gifts, opening advent calendars, going on out-ings to hear choirs sing carols — Austin sank deeper in work. He tried to distance himself from Noah a bit, and his job seemed an easy way to do it. But whenever they did talk, it was all business as before, and when Noah had let himself in a few evenings back, they slept together, and it was, to be fair, really good. That night was the firm's Christmas party and Austin was still in the office even as his colleagues began to shuffle out.

'I'll see you at the do tonight, then, ya?' Nelson did the weird thing of popping his head over Austin's cubicle so that his torso looked disconnected from the rest of his body. It was reminiscent of one of Dickens' ghosts of Christmas, or maybe dead Marley, especially this time of time.

'No, I won't be there.' Austin didn't bother to look up as he clipped off these words in the general direction of Nelson's pie hole.

Nelson stood silent and confused. Everyone went to the firm's holiday party. It was an unwritten rule that the more senior members of staff were to buy the more junior ones extra beers when their three company-issued drink coupons ran out. QCs would buy for clerks, senior members would buy for junior members, and juniors for pupils. Nelson had been counting on Austin's generosity.

'It's at seven, so you can wrap up here and go,' he said, hoping Austin was playing at coy.

'Listen,' Austin said finally looking up, 'I said I'm not going. I arranged last week with her solicitor to see Etta Daniels. Getting her a plea bargain has taken a considerable amount of effort.'

Nelson stared, baffled.

'You remember Ms James? She's one of those *lovely* clients we're helping for free.'

'Ya, but,' Nelson gave Austin one of his most earnest smiles, 'plea bargaining is easy for someone of your calibre.' He thought flattery would get him everywhere.

'Except the guidelines set by the Sentencing Council require that the abatement given to the sentence is determined by the timing of the plea and no other factors.'

Nelson stood deadpan.

'Christ. Did you even go to law school?' Austin rose from his chair and came out from the cubicle. He stood shoulder-to-shoulder with Nelson now. 'In simple terms: the guidelines state that the earlier the guilty plea is entered, the greater the discount to the sentence.'

'Oh, and you waited too long with this one?'

'Something like that,' Austin said and put his hand on his head as he returned to his desk. 'Off you go now, Nelson. Enjoy the party.'

The truth was that Austin did not have to stay in the office past seven, but his mind was on more important pursuits than a collegial gathering of yuletide cheer at a local pub. Noah had bought tickets to a West End play and surprised Austin with them the day before. Having grown up with the film Grease, singing 'There are worse things I could do, than go with a boy or two ...' at the top of his lungs, Austin was excited about the lead.

Stockard Channing was playing Kristin Miller, an art historian who struggles with balancing a love of work with the complex relationships she has with her two grown children, both of whom feel she neglected them. In the way he appeared at the theatre, it would be easy to imagine Noah as one of these two children, for he very much looked neglected. His raggedy t-shirt did much to show off his muscular biceps but very little to keep him warm on a cold December night. Austin thought he spotted one or two holes in his chinos as well. For someone that once floated so effortlessly cool, Noah looked drained.

They had the cheap seats — not the ones at the back of the dress circle that can be bought for a little bit of money quite early on, but the ones in the very front row labelled AA which you get at the last minute for fifteen or twenty pounds. A very elongated neck is a requirement for such a seat given you're sitting at an angle below the actors on stage. Nonetheless, the show proved worth every bit of the forty pounds Noah spent, which Austin imagined a considerable sum for Noah's shallow pockets.

A particularly poignant scene saw Channing dive into a soliloquy when asked why the focus of her scholarship is on Giotto and not some other, more popular artist such as Michelangelo or da

Vinci. Any understanding of art today must, in fact, begin with Giotto, she asserts. He made a decisive break with the prevalent Byzantine style of the late Middle Ages and in doing so, ushered in what would become the Renaissance of great Western painting. Giotto revolutionised the technique of drawing accurately from life, which had been neglected for more than two hundred years before his time. This is her Apologia, also the title of the play, and by definition a defence of the character's life choices. Not an apology, as she is quite clear she has nothing to for which to apologise. Noah and Austin left the theatre that evening in awe of Channing's mesmerising performance and full of curiosity about Giotto, a name neither one of them had heard before.

The next morning, the Saturday skies opened up to bright yellow rays after a tumultuous night of thunder storms. As they walked down the roads of Maida Vale, Noah stared in wonder at the saplings in this part of the city. Most of them were evergreen trees and even in the bleak seasons kept their shimmering green hues. The foliage in his own neighbourhood was sparse and browning in comparison.

Austin shook his head and smiled, 'They're just trees, babe.'

But Noah carried on about it all the way to Charing Cross Station, and when they alighted the tube, Austin said 'They're just trees' again only to belabour this obvious point.

Even at ten-thirty in the morning, the National Gallery was full of tourists. It had been Austin's idea to come here. He developed such a fascination with Renaissance art in the hours since the play that he spent a good forty-five minutes googling where to see Giotto in London. Pushing through throngs of poorly-dressed people speaking dozens of languages all sounding like gobbledygook in their collective chaos, he soon regretted the decision. But he had a clear plan in mind: push through to the Sainsbury Wing.

Room 51 has the earliest works in the National Gallery, from the 13th and 14th centuries, and among them are two works by Giotto. Noah, to Austin's surprise, spotted the first of them, Pentecost (c 1310). In the painting's foreground, men from various nations stand in awe at hearing the words of the Twelve Apostles spoken in their own native dialects.

They stood for a long time a few feet from the painting. Austin ground the soles of his shoes hard onto the parquet floors and dawned a serious face. He marvelled at the aesthetics of the picture.

'See, Noah, what the Stockard Channing character went on about is absolutely right,' he said with his nose now a few centimetres from the wooden panel on which Pentecost is painted. 'The figures are not stylised or elongated; they are solid and three-dimensional. I mean look, even the spectators in the front of the canvas have real faces and make real gestures.' He waved his hands to mimic the subjects. 'Even the garments hang naturally and have form and weight.'

When he looked over to Noah, he expected to find him listening blankly or to be fiddling with his phone. Instead, Noah wept. Small, but observable tears.

'What is it?' Austin asked.

'It's so damn beautiful,' Noah said, his eyes never leaving the canvas.

What had been left unsaid was that the diversity of the figures and the way the Holy Spirit is shown descending on the apostles in the form of a dove reminded him of the Islamic concept Ruh al-Qudus — the source of prophetic revelation. In Shia Islam, Imams and Prophets received messages from Al-Quddus, the Holy Spirit. But while Prophets were able to see the Holy Spirit, the Imams could only hear the messages in dreams.

'It is stunning,' said Austin. He allowed himself a tiny bit of pride at their new-found mutual interest.

The Uber pulled into the departures wing of Terminal 3, Heathrow Airport at two o'clock. Their flight was at two-forty-five and Austin hated being late. This was also one of the things he had grown to dislike most about Noah in the three months since they'd been together — his seemingly compulsive need to run behind schedule.

The day had started pleasantly enough. Austin woke at half eight, percolated a cup of Joe, and opened the New York Times travel section to read its Things To Do in Florence article.

'Here's what you do first in Florence ... Complain about the tourists.' Austin thought there was little chance of that. It was late December and he'd booked an exclusive hotel somewhat off the beaten path for their Christmas and New Year's Eve holiday. It was to be perfect. Since Noah didn't celebrate Christmas, Austin used it as an opportunity to get away from blistery England. The five-star accommodation butted against the Arno but still had easy access to the Uffizi and other major attractions. This had been a point of contention between them, Noah preferring some-thing more central, less posh, and therefore presumably cheaper than the seven-hundred pound per night St Regis.

The one thing they agreed on was seeing as much Giotto as possible. The master had lived and worked in Florence, lending his hand to the design of the campanile and leaving bits and pieces of his frescoes and paintings dotting the region.

It was on the back of the inspirational trip to the National that Austin booked this trip. Now stood in the security check queue, everything about the airport experience irritated him. This was only exacerbated by Noah having made them late on account of waiting until noon to pack his bag. And that was another thing. Austin packed a diligent hold-all while Noah threw his things into a rucksack. 'Not exactly St Regis appropriate, is it?' Austin snarked as Noah tossed the bag into the back of the Prius. Now everyone's choice of luggage annoyed him. The Adidas gym bags carried by the wannabe footballers and the old school suitcases rolled by the grannies — it all made Austin cringe.

They spent the majority of the two-hour flight ignoring each other, so it was little wonder the cab ride from Firenze Airport to the banks of the

Arno was filled with angst. For his part, Austin tried to lighten the mood by suggesting they browse the guidebook for a restaurant in which to have dinner. But Noah would have none of it. The damage had been done and he spent the cab ride, as well as duration of the hotel check-in, sulking.

The light from the next morning's Christmas Eve sun pierced the blinds of the hotel room, promising a clean slate and a full day of gallery browsing. At breakfast, Noah spoke few words opting instead to read a local newspaper. But Austin chalked this up to fatigue and refused to believe Noah could still be brooding from their tiff the day before.

In this small place, with its streets laid out in right angles and a fountain at every block, the duo walked in deliberation. Although it was their first visit, there seemed to be a familiarity to Florence that each of them sensed without expressing it to the other. With its iconic cathedral dome and gentle, rolling hills, for Austin this was a place of majesty and a symbol of power. It was the amber wheat fields, silver olive groves, and absinthe-green vineyards he could see from a distance surrounding the old town that spoke to Noah.

Opposite the Ponte Vecchio, Austin pulled Noah into a small stationary shop. Words seemed of little use, so he didn't bother asking Noah if he'd like to go but towed him in by the cusp of his jumper. It was a shop of no more than twenty shelves built of polished stone like medieval store cupboards. Above, on the painted white ceiling, a relief ornament in the shape of a wreath with five red balls surrounding it had been plastered over. Despite its grandiose appearance, the shop sold the tat tourists grew to hate and simultaneously expect in that strange cycle of supply and demand. Austin picked up a small notepad with the phrase I Heart Florence on the cover. He began to understand somewhere between Heathrow and the Uffizi that he had lost touch with Noah and needed to refocus. He had ambitions of the two of them filling those cut-rate pages with short poems inspired by some combination of the winter sun and Renaissance painting.

Then there was the art. About three hundred metres away from the inadequate bookshop was heaven and it went by the name of the Uffizi. In late December, this grand museum wore its finest winter cloak. Marble-glazed halls welcomed tourists and art-lovers alike with open arms. As Noah set off to see The Birth of the Venus, Austin put one goal in mind: to visit all 13,000 square metres. Alas the long, narrow hallways which open to vistas of the Arno and the roads below articulated the space of the gallery so perfectly that Austin soon realised this was an impossible mission. He would, instead, focus on the Late Medieval galleries.

The first lines Austin wrote in his new notebook were not verse but critique, which he copied diligently from a small plasterboard next to a painting: 'Giotto's work was a return to a more classic way of depicting the human as the main focal point.'

Austin filled the little notebook that day. He made lists of the names and dates of paintings he liked. He drew rough sketches of the David. He described streets and the people inhabiting them. But not a single page contained a poem. He chalked this up to the argument with Noah, who was still, despite Austin's attempts to smooth things over, not speaking in more than short responses. The notebook became a chronicle of their first full day in Florence, all from only Austin's perspective. By sunset he had spent more time engaging with those pages than he'd spent speaking to his boyfriend. (Boyfriend? Is that what he is?)

They sat for a late dinner in the hotel restaurant. Noah spent the duration of the time it took to eat the starters and mains sending text messages to someone.

'Be cool. It's just my sister,' he said.

This was more than he'd said since the airport, but the lack of table manners peeved Austin who was left to stare into space contemplating. It occurred to him, not without cause, that Noah's emotional state was two-faced. He could be incredibly charming and articulate when it suited him, but when his ego was bruised, he would revert into himself like a snail crawling into its shell. True, Austin had not gone easy on Noah over packing nor at running late for the airport. But it was also true that Noah's response had been disproportionate. Austin tried to engage Noah in small talk and picked-up the tab not only for the hotel — as he promised to do — but also for all their cab rides, meals, and museum tickets. He was starting to feel used: Noah would mumble no more than a curt 'cheers' as though he expected Austin, as the bigger earner, to pay the way. This, coupled with the lack of communication, only served to heighten Austin's anxiety.

As dessert was served, Noah's shell broke not unlike the way he crushed the meringue engulfed by strawberries and cream. 'I just keep thinking,' he said, startling Austin out of daydreaming, 'you care more about the art at the Uffizi than you do about this relationship or even about me.'

Austin dropped his spoon and stared at Noah. 'What do you want from me?'

'I want you to stop trying to make me into a goddamn Giotto fresco. I'm not your bloody Renaissance. I'm not perfect.'

Austin wanted to walk away, but as he began to push back the chair from the table, he remembered his mother having left him as a ten-year-old at the supper table one evening when she became annoyed with his incessant rundown of the school day — What kind of rice is this? I asked the lunch lady. Do you know what my teacher said in Maths? Jimmy told Justin on the playground that Tina is a bad speller. Well Mrs Hirlea said she could have it back if she asked nicely and do you know what she said? — and he resolved then to neither treat Noah as a child nor to relive that shame on him.

Grasping the edges of the table, Austin spoke slowly: 'Those pictures have more life in them than you ever show, Noah —'

'And the stupid notebook ...'

'You want to know why I paid so much attention to the notebook and to those paintings? Because you pay no attention to me.'

Noah looked up from the meringue. 'What?'

'You haven't said two words to me since the airport. The notebook? That's something I thought we'd share together. You know, write down the names of pictures we saw, things to look up later. I thought it'd be like the West End and National Gallery all over again.'

'And that's the whole reason we came here.'

'Yes!' Austin thought there'd been a break-through. 'That is the whole reason.'

'Well I'm sorry to have disappointed you, mate.' And with that, Noah pushed back his chair and left the dinner table.

On Christmas morning, Austin awoke early and stared at the sugary array of stars dazzling the early morning sky over the Arno. He opened the window to let in a bit of fresh air; the breeze blew weightless against his bare arms. He imagined this was the way it would always feel in Florence if he'd never had a row with the man still sleeping in the bed.

Sipping on water to quell his anxiety, Austin gently shook Noah from his slumber. 'Happy Christmas, babe, it's time to get up.'

Noah grumbled and put a pillow over his face. 'But it's still dark outside.'

'The day is young and fresh and full of possibility.' This optimism was new to Austin, and he wondered where it came from. 'Let's watch the sunrise.'

He heaved Noah out of bed and onto the miniature balcony of their hotel room. Within a few minutes time, they began to detect subtle changes in the sky to the east. The firmament in the opposite direction sat still dark, but over the river an assortment of yellow and orange on the horizon fell beneath an opaque blue ocean of night that was beginning to evaporate. The outlines of trees and rooflines below grew shadowy.

Austin pulled himself into Noah sucking up the warmness radiating from his body. About twenty minutes later, daybreak became more glorious as the sun peeked over the horizon. The sky now became pink with cotton candy and as the sun ascended higher into the morning, the western skyline glimmered with neon.

The intrepid air of dawn on Christmas sparked something wonderful in Austin, and it wasn't long before he coaxed Noah out onto the deserted streets of the city. They roamed between courtyards and alleyways, the Florence of Dante, and one could imagine nothing had or ever could change there.

Of course, every Christmas is a quarantine of sorts. We lock ourselves in with family and friends, sometimes long-lost connections we've reacquainted with, sometimes close relatives we wish would vanish. Shops close-up and the only restaurants open have no free tables. When it's only you and a handful of other tourists on empty roads, you can be forgiven for indulging in a little bit of ego-boosting. So, as they approached the Palazzo Vecchio, Austin got the idea they ought to have a photo in front of the grand reproduction of Michelangelo's David, and he solicited one of the few other tourists to snap it. Realising he'd forgotten his phone in the hotel, he asked for Noah's.

Noah wearily obliged, but all the while harboured hard feelings. The grim combination of his bruised ego, lack of easy access to stimulants, and Austin's exuberance boiled through him on the inside. As the eyes of David, with a warning glare, were turned towards Rome so were Noah's toward to Austin. 'Do not come closer,' their silent cry.

'I can't do this. I have to go,' he said at last, facing Austin as they turned down a side street in search of lunch.

Austin, no doubt used to Noah's sudden and odd behaviour, smiled with confusion. 'What's that?'

'It's this place, today, my nerves ...'. None of these justifications sounded quite right, even to Noah.

'But babe, it's Christmas. Try to be happy, yes?' Austin patted Noah on the back.

'I need to some air,' Noah said and began to jog off in the opposite direction.

As he scurried off, Noah wondered if this had been the best way to break the news to Austin. Had it been clear he couldn't pretend any longer? That he needed to do more work on himself, or that he couldn't even fathom doing that work — didn't have the will or desire to? It's funny to ask yourself these questions when all you really want is to get high. Does addiction wait for Christmas then? No. Not when he could easily find a dealer on Craigslist just by pulling out his phone. When he at last returned to the hotel that evening, Austin had already turned in for the night. Noah collapsed on the sofa, waking the next morning to find Austin had already dressed and gone out. A note on the bureau invited Noah to join him for lunch.

Roaming the alleys of a Medieval city can be a strange and lonesome affair when you're on your own. When Austin sat out that morning, the brightness of Florence that existed just a day before vanished and, in its place, a cold drizzle emerged. Dragging on for hours, he felt it would never end. Among the roads where giants from Machiavelli to Galileo trod, Austin morphed into a stranger at odds not only with the city, but with himself. A sickness hung over him. His muscles ached, the trace of a cough emerged. Even in his down jacket and heavy scarf, chills blathered through his veins.

When Austin returned to the hotel just before lunchtime, he was surprised to see Noah in the lobby wearing his rucksack and too busy in mid-conversation with the receptionist to notice anyone approach.

'No, bro, you listen here,' Noah said, his hands flailing, 'it's only *me* checking out, just me. The other one is staying on.'

An indecipherable fear gripped him, and Austin ducked out the door of the hotel and hid around the corner for what seemed like a very long twenty minutes.

On the last day of December, Austin sat on the small balcony of his flat and gazed at the rooftops of chilly Northwest London. It was a far cry from Florence, where he'd planned to celebrate the dawn of a new year, but he wasn't complaining. After Noah's early departure and his own solo plane ride home back to the U.K., Austin needed nothing more than to sit here with his cup of coffee and very English view. A line of poetry floated through this head: *Our whisper woke no clocks, We kissed and I was glad, at everything you did.* It was

Zara who first introduced him to this little gem by Auden.

After he flew back from Florence, Zara collected him from the airport and drove him to a tiny gastropub outside of Horley. There, they ordered a bottle of cheap prosecco and collapsed on an old sofa. He knew then things were over with Noah, but he couldn't squarely explain why. When Zara asked for some backstory, a piece of evidence, if you will, she could use to understand how it had gotten to that point, all Austin could say was 'I guess people make mistakes.'

'But what mistakes did he make, Aus.?'

'No, it was I who made the mistake, Z., me. I should never have gotten mixed up with someone like him.'

A pile of bills and a stack of newspapers each marked with the passing of days waited for Austin as he stumbled over them into Flat 83. Noah's note sat there too, tucked inside Car Magazine between an advertisement for the new Bentley and a feature on 'the perfect luggage for weekend country drives.' Something struck Austin about the apparent randomness of the note having been placed there between pages twenty-six and twenty-seven. Noah had always had a thing for luxury cars and never went anywhere without his tattered rucksack. Although undated, the note couldn't have been there for more than a few hours. The paper still reeked with the slight smell of ammonia left by the pen's ink. In perfect cursive:

> *You left me no choice. I wanted to talk to you, to tell you how I felt but I couldn't find the right words. This is tough for me, you know, leaving you like this. I'll post the key. Keep whatever I left behind, if you want. I can't love you anymore. Guess I never really did. Don't hate me.*
> *Noah xx*

Prying himself off the balcony, Austin ripped the note in half and threw it over the edge. He reached for his iPhone and scrolled to Noah's number, first on the list. His index finger poised to stab the call button, but he stopped short of pressing down. He closed his eyes, took a breath, and held it a moment. What could he say to him? Numbness crept over Austin, warm and comforting. He nodded to himself, reassured by the rulebook racing through his brain. He put the phone back in its case and sat staring at his knees.

Fifteen minutes later, still sitting in the same place, Austin came out of his paralysis. He pulled the mobile out of his pocket again and this time didn't hesitate to dial Noah's number.

'Hey,' came the answer.

Austin's complexion turned ruddy. 'What the hell, Noah! You leave me that immature note and now you answer the phone "hey" like nothing has happened!'

'What do you want me to say?' Noah's flat voice asked.

'I want you to explain yourself, to explain this note, to explain why you think I left you no choice but to leave me in the lurch like this ...' Austin's words faltered as tears crept into the corners of his eyelids.

'That's the problem, Austin. You always want explanations. You can't take anything at face value, everything has to be explained, everything has to be your way.'

'Can't you just answer the question, babe?' Austin didn't mean to call him that — this pet name they'd developed, like so many other couples, early on. But old habits die hard.

'I can't speak to you right now. Not when you're like this. Key is in the post.' And with that Noah hung up.

The phone screen again displayed Austin's list of contacts. He began scrolling through the entries. Who does one turn to when the prospect of speaking to anyone at all feels sickening? The Ms contained a single entry: Mum / Millicent. It struck him as odd seeing it now written that way. Don't most people just put Mummy or Mother? It seemed almost schizophrenic to write it that way. She was Mum when either or the both of them were on good behaviour, and Millicent when one of them (her, inevitably her) misbehaved. And don't all children have this awkward love-hate relationship with their parents? Did Noah? He felt he might lose the plot and willed himself to press that strange combined entry.

The doorbell rang as Austin began to pour his second cup of coffee. Moments later his mother greeted him at the door. He found he didn't want the caffeine now. The thought of her presence alone had been all the jolt he needed. He invited her through to the balcony. Outside the sun was rising and the haze of the yellow and white beams helped to calm Austin's nerves.

'Are you okay, my boy?' she said and stroked his hair as if he were a child again.

She drank her cuppa and he stared at the tops of houses and trees, both of them preoccupied with their own thoughts. It is okay like this, he thought, her presence is enough; we don't need to speak. He invited her, she hadn't come unannounced, so why was he so disturbed by her company?

But after some time, he grew weary and an image of a Giotto fresco sat on his mind. His face creased in intensity as he pictured Judas kissing Jesus, at once erotic and friendly, but which is in fact harmful to the recipient. It was The Betrayal of Christ (1305) and it moved him now in a way it hadn't done in person. And paintings are like that, he thought, they stick with you and shape you long after you've forgotten how they look.

'But what's the shelf-life of a relationship?' asked Austin suddenly.

'It's the same as the shelf-life of a fact,' his mother said. Questions out of context did not strike her off-guard.

'Uh, facts are immutable.'

He looked down to the street below. The road was nearly empty. It looked strange, too, Austin sitting there with his mother and her very loud, very American accent beaming over the subtle lightness of an otherwise peaceful morning.

'Ever the lawyer,' she said, and took a sip of her now-cooling coffee. 'No, facts can change. New evidence comes to light, your understanding shifts. The facts change. Knowledge is morphing all the time. New facts replace old ones, more precise measurements come about.' The directness of her tone could take a philosophical turn when she had something of importance to say. That was one thing he knew he inherited from her. 'What was once considered true is overturned daily. It's the same with relationships; they have an expiration date.'

'But not all of them, right? Some last forever. When you find the right one.'

'Nothing lasts forever,' she said taking another sip from her mug. 'Death comes, sooner or later.'

Coffee had a chameleon-like effect on Austin's mother. Though it is the consummate non-prescription upper it can also be a balm, a salve. He thought her unduly pessimistic, but no matter what counterpoint he offered up, his mother always returned to this bottom line. And he wanted to admit she was on to something. But there's always a backdoor, he thought. Children, even grown ones, rarely like to admit their parents are right.

'That's so ghastly, mum.' It was settled; he could call her Mum today.

'Listen, sometimes beauty is found in the downright unpleasantness of life. It's about survival, kid.' — Austin looked up, unaccustomed now to being called a kid. — 'That's how relationships work, by which I mean how they don't work, don't come to be. You get so comfortable, and he takes advantage of everything you've given him; maybe not consciously, but that's the result.

You've given your attention. Some people give their money. Your time. All of that just for the relationship to be over in three weeks, two months, whatever. You have already poured out all your emotions. You guys talk on the phone. You are texting. You already feel for him, but he leaves you hanging. And you're still there thinking it's something.'

'That's kind of heart-breaking, isn't it? Even if it was only a short amount of time.'

He trusted her words came in part from the abrupt ending to the relationship with his father, something they never spoke of directly. She was obviously still hurt, more than thirty years later.

For her part, her views on parenting had changed in the more than three decades since she gave birth to Austin. She once thought she needed to prepare him for the world; this was her job as a parent. But now she believed it was to protect him from the world and all that is out there. All the heartbreak and lies and madmen and hurt.

'But this is the reality of the situation. Even though the guy sounds nice, sometimes says the right things, no, this dude is going through some shit, just like you. You want to believe this person is the right one for you, but probably they're not. So, you just end up being messed about eventually, by your own emotions and your regret at having jumped in too soon ... If you want my advice, this is it: Distract yourself.'

When Austin set-off in the evening to do just that, he couldn't understand all his mother wanted was for him to acknowledge her being. She would have liked to sit all day like that, watching the sun rise and then set, sipping one coffee after another, talking or not. They might discuss her considerable knowledge of men, or his work, or Zara's penchant for acting like she were Austin's older sister (something they could agree on) — any or all of this would be a way towards saying *We are family, we love each other.* But ten o'clock came and she left.

Noah turned up unexpectedly on New Year's Eve at his parents' home. Didn't he have plans for the evening? they asked. No, he said, and failed to tell them he was meant to be in Florence, but it had all gone wrong. Now sat in the lounge of the family house, images of his childhood came floating back to Noah. The turn of the year has a way of reviving brain cells.

Noah's earliest reliable memory was of the long, white sheet. He was eight-years-old, and his mother put it on him on a rainy Friday morning.

'It's called a thobe,' she said and then put a little white cap on his head. She called that a taqiyah. These were the things he wore to Friday prayer from that week onwards until the third month of his seventeenth year.

'Why aren't you dressed?' asked Lilly when she saw her son descend from the upper floor of their home that Friday, 'Are you ill?'

'No, I'm just giving up.'

'Giving what up?'

'The outfit, wearing the thobe and all. It's not for me.'

This was the first sign of trouble.

True, most young men no longer wore their white robes and prayer caps to mosque; it wasn't a requirement. But Lilly's son was not meant to be like most boys. She always imagined there was something special in him, something resourceful that would set him on a path for success out of Northeast London.

One can imagine Lilly's dismay when Noah dropped out of university after only half a term. 'I'm getting a job,' he announced. Aashirbaad didn't put up a fight, happy as he was so long as Noah paid his own way. And so, it had been settled. He moved out of the family home within a week and took everything but his now too-small thobe with him. It was when she went to clean his room for the first time after the move that Lilly discovered the thin, white paper wrappers. She knew some people rolled their own tobacco, she'd seen some of her husband's friends smoking those types of cigarettes. But Lilly was no fool. For one thing, she never once saw Noah smoke, nor had she smelled it on him. And this was not cigarette rolling paper, it was cigar paper, the type used to make blunts.

Now in such situations, a mother has a choice. It a choice made out of necessity more than anything else. She can notify the father of the child to deal with the situation, or she can deal with it herself. Option number one risks the chance the father might not do anything at all, and that's why this was never an option for Lilly. Men are like that, she surmised, lazy unless it suits them. But option number two also had its downsides: children rarely listen to their mothers. It was an odd thing about boys — and she ought to know having had three of them — they demand all of your attention when they are hurting, when they need something; but when they've done wrong, they hide, they deny, they outright lie. Anything to avoid admitting their mother is right. And so, she let it go. It's a phase, he'll grow out of it. Inaction was the simplest course of action. And ordinarily, she might have been right. Many a young adult smokes up once, twice, even a dozen times and then lets it go. What Lilly could never have anticipated, and could never have been blamed for, was that the marijuana had been but a gateway for her eldest son.

Five, Four, Three, Two, One. Happy New Year! But not for Lilly. She watched as her son let out the softest of tears. He was hurting. When a child hurts, so does his mother.

Sunday morning. The first day of the new year. Austin fumbled out of bed at eleven after a night of light drinking, heavy smoking, and very little conversation. He'd known since he about twenty-one that even a little bit of alcohol has magnified effects when mixed with tobacco. The more fags, the deeper the hangover. And last night was no exception, save his intention to forget Noah for one night, preferably by meeting some other equally attractive, if not intellectually stimulating, man and hooking up. One red-hot night. But now he swam in vacuousness, having met no one and having spent the majority of the evening transferring from the bar to the smoking terrace and back.

Austin planned to meet Zara at eleven-thirty in St Albans, the dormitory suburb a forty-five-minute commute from his flat. He threw on a t-shirt, jumper, and a pair of crumpled jeans, laced up some old sneakers and flew out the door. It occurred to him not for the first time that week that his personal hygiene and fashion sense were on a steady decline in the days since Noah left him.

Arriving half an hour late and annoyed at himself, Austin spotted Zara at the back corner of Bill's Restaurant reading a book. God, she must be pissed at me, he thought, but she looked up and smiled. 'I know it's hard these days, Austin. Don't beat yourself up for being late.' She looked at him with empathy, the kind only a friend who's been there and done that can have.

'I think there's something wrong with me, Z. My emotions are all off kilter.'

'Of course, there is, Austin. Noah left you.' — Fuck, she thought, I don't want to be harsh — 'I'm sorry. I care for you and I want you to know it's okay to feel out of sorts right now.' She gave him a warm smile, and when she did her pleasant, oyster-white teeth lit up the room.

'I know, and thanks, but it's not just him. I've been having a dream. I used to have it all the time, and then I guess it went away for a while, and now it's back like an old lover, one I never wanted to see again.'

'Where do you think this dream comes from? What are its roots, its sources?' asked Zara, taking a sip of her cortado.

'The dream is old. The memory feels new,' Austin said.

'How do you mean?'

'A few years ago, I started to have a recurring dream about a wall of fire a few hundred feet high coming toward me. It felt like a rogue wave on the sea, an ocean of fire. I couldn't escape. Sometimes I would look to run in the other direction, only to see a wall of fire coming from there as well. Not sure what this was, but quite vivid. Thought I was prophetic. Glad I was wrong.' It was unusual for Austin to equivocate in such a choppy manner.

'Why do you think you stopped having the dream?' Zara wondered.

'Noah. Because of Noah. See, my aunt died in a house fire on Christmas Eve when I was around fourteen years old. It had a tremendous impact on me. Don't think I ever recovered from it. I saw what it did to my grandmother, knowing her daughter's life had been extinguished.'

'That must have been incredibly tough.' — Her heart ached at the thought. — 'Do you think the dream was some manifestation of that?'

'It's possible. Just a few days ago I read the comments on a random Twitter post. Some

@somethingoranother wrote "go die in a fire" in the comments section. Evidently, he didn't like what the poster had to say. I think of all the expressions brandished around the Internet these days, "go die in a fire" is the one I like the least.'

'That's understandable,' said Zara.

Austin went on: 'When my aunt died, I became almost fascinated with what happened to her. It wasn't morbid. I just needed to understand what it all meant. I mean our Christmas that year and every year after was pretty much soured. Did you know when someone is caught in a fire, the first thing that happens is the hair and skin start to burn? Imagine the smell. The skin cracks, body hair singes off. The coroner told my grandmother that Aunt Mary had gone quickly. Had felt no pain. But this can't be true. He might have been trying to spare gran's feelings. In truth, all the nerve endings start going off kinetically, shouting at you through a thick veil of pain to get out of harm's way. But you can't and as your body gets hotter and hotter, the layer of fat under the skin starts to give in. And the eyes. Your eyelids are just a thin sheet of tissue, so they will melt off with speed. But the eyeball will liquify. It will boil and then burst, and only then will it burn away.'

'Jesus. You don't have to go on,' Zara said, sweeping pools of jaundiced hair away from her face.

'No, I need to. It's only at this point that if you're lucky and have a low tolerance for pain, you might become unconscious. But I know Aunt Mary was never lucky. She had a hard life, always working as a waitress or a cleaner or some other job like that while the rest of her seven siblings had successful careers and children, big houses and all that. So, I just think she wouldn't have been lucky to go that fast. She would have lived long enough to watch her own body fall apart. The worst part is that the larynx is one of the body's more protected areas, surrounded by muscle and cartilage, so Mary could still have screamed. Even after her hair and skin flaked off and her eyes dissolved, she would have been calling out for help. No, she wasn't lucky. Not unless the universe decided at the last minute to give her a reprieve.'

Some time passed as they both sat in silence, Zara staring at the back cover of her book and Austin's eyes glazed over.

'A few weeks after my aunt died, I saw my gran cooking beef stew on the hob. She broke down crying and wailing just as the pot began to boil. Maybe she knew that human protein and muscle tissue cook away like a cow's do. The internal organs boil and explode and if the fire is intense enough, eventually everything dries up, withers, and fades away.'

'Does that frighten you?' asked Zara.

'No. It empowers me,' said Austin, his voice flat.

'Death empowers you?'

'Not death, not precisely. A dream is nothing but a want or a desire in life. An object, a person, something missing. I think I'm missing the kind of love my grandmother had for my Aunt Mary. The kind that hurts to the core.'

'I think that's the kind of love that only comes from having children,' Zara offered.

'I used to think that, but not anymore. Desire can be created or inspired by someone else or some thing. I wanted it with Noah. And I stopped dreaming about the tsunami of fire shortly after he came into my life.'

Austin met Zara again at ten the next Thursday morning on Westferry Road, near his office. It had become, in some comically macabre way, a biannual ritual of theirs. They'd visit the STD clinic together, each having the rapid HIV blood test in separate rooms, then waiting together in the lobby for the thirty or so minutes it took to get the results. Afterwards, they'd go for a late breakfast and feel oddly smug at having done their duty as good people knowing their sexual health status.

It would happen occasionally, on days like this one, that the clinic was full, and Zara and Austin would be called separately to have their fingers pricked. It also happened that Zara was meeting a potential new investor at the art gallery she managed in Whitechapel and so she said her goodbyes to Austin at ten-thirty-five just after receiving the usual negative results of the test, leaving Austin in the waiting room with last month's GQ and a promise to meet up next weekend for drinks.

The clinic was an unpredictable place. All could, and usually did, go well and you'd be out in half an hour. On other days, the wait was twenty minutes to be called, another fifteen to see a phlebotomist, and another forty-five for results. But you'd never think much of it, aware this was how the National Health Service worked. But as the clock approached eleven-thirty that morning, Austin began to wonder what was taking quite so long. The waiting room thinned out and the reception staff passed the time without so many patients by gabbing and laughing with each other around one of the workstations, presumably looking at some YouTube video or Facebook meme.

Patience in the face of perceived laziness had never been one of Austin's strengths. Approaching the reception desk, annoyed and running behind schedule, he addressed the first employee to look up: 'I'm still waiting on my results. My test was near an hour ago already.'

'Name?' the receptionist replied curtly. Austin gave his, with the exact same brusqueness.

'Ah, umm-hmm,' the receptionist said flipping through a stack of papers attached to a clipboard, 'just a moment; I'll find someone to call you back.'

Austin sat for another few minutes until a broad-shouldered woman called his name from the corridor opposite the reception desk. Her uniform struck Austin as odd. Test results were normally delivered by a trainee nurse or healthcare assistant dressed in all green scrubs. This woman was a fully-qualified nurse or lab technician. She wore tailored trousers and a fitted top with a white lab coat which helped to soften her imposing stance. She led Austin to a small consultation room no bigger than a walk-through closet. 'Please have a seat, sir. Can I get you a cup of water?' He'd never known the staff at this clinic to be exceptionally polite. Never rude, but certainly not so accommodating. His first thought was to tense into self-righteousness, thinking they were trying to make it up to him for the long wait. But as he sat, turning down the water, Austin's heart began to beat like the rhythm of a hip-hop song. Get a grip, man. He steeled himself and smiled uneasily as the woman sat down in the chair opposite, a small white table separating them. All this white — so sterile, so nacreous. It began to elicit panic.

'Is this your first HIV test, sir?' The woman's face looked kind. Too kind. Austin's palms leaked sweat.

'You can call me Austin. No, it's okay, I get them every six months, so you can skip the provisos about what you tested, the two different types of HIV, and so forth.'

'Right, Austin, ... so I have the results of your test here. When was the last time you were tested?'

'Must have been around summer of last year. It was negative, like always.'

'I'm afraid that's not the case today, Austin.'

The remainder of the conversation became a blur. Dreams often involve elements from our waking lives — people we've encountered, familiar locations — but they take on a fantastical cadence. Night terrors cause people to scream, to bolt out of bed, or to have panic attacks. Not to be confused with nightmares, which can leave unpleasant memories or can cause mild anxiety, night terrors are usually not remembered the next day, even though the dreamer may appear to be awake during the experience. This is how the conversation went down in Austin's mind. A night terror, but one for which he was awake.

Many people report in their scariest of dreams, locations shift or blend with one another. The actors and plot take on absurd, impossible, or contradictory elements. If you were to ask Austin to describe the moment in the twenty-five-square foot all-white room where he learned that he was HIV-positive, he'd tell you that everything happened in slow motion. But the truth is he remembered none of what the broad-shouldered nurse said apart from You Have It. He would remember running as fast as he could out of the clinic, moving with lightning speed while his surroundings moved slowly and methodically out of sync. He tried to scream, but no sound came out. This also often happened when he was terrified of something in his dreams. Dreaming/reality. A blurred line.

In something of a daydream, Austin walked aimlessly for the next quarter of an hour from Westferry Road to West India Quay, pacing up and down pavement, trying to think what to do next. He lost all sense of time and then stopped caring he was late for work or behind schedule. When he came to a cafe sandwiched between the high-rises of Canary Wharf, he ordered a cappuc-cino, sat in the corner of the shop and wept.

After a few minutes of silent, but steady crying, Austin's tear ducts dried. He sat stone-faced staring into the black screen of his mobile. Dialling Zara, he wondered what to say if she picked up. They never spoke on the phone, preferring text messages to vocal conversation which required time out of whatever else one was doing. After three rings, he figured she wouldn't answer but just as he was ready to hang-up, the receiver clicked.

'Hey, Austin, pleasant surprise!' Zara said. 'Did you miss me that much?'

Her enthusiasm sent Austin into a fit of tears, and before he could manage to utter a single word, Zara knew. She'd had her suspicions for months, thinking Austin's recent bout with the flu might have been some early sign of seroconversion. And she'd never thought Austin to be a very good judge of character. Too eager to be loved, and therefore willing to believe whoever would make fake promises of fidelity and assurances of their health. But still she did not judge nor pity him. She let Austin cry and consoled him with the gentle reassurance he was not alone, that he could live a normal life with the right treatment. But Austin did not cry because he thought he would die. He cried because he understood he would live. He would live with this thing for as long as he lived. He would re-live the instance every day of his life, and he would be forced to make others live it vicariously — every close friend, every lover, every person he chose to tell would be forced to deal with this transgression.

Zara implored him gently, 'The first step is to get help, Austin.'

'I know, I know,' he said. 'The clinic made an appointment for me at the Chelsea and Westminster Hospital for next week.'

'That's good, but I don't mean just getting the meds. You need to talk to someone, a professional.'

'You mean another shrink, Z.,' Austin said.

'I mean someone to help you process what's happening, to start accepting it. You told me a while ago you think something is wrong with your emotions, and I am scared this is going to deepen that fear. You have to figure out how you contracted it and what you can do differently next time around.'

'Well I already know how I got it ...' he replied quietly. 'It's Noah.'

Seventy-two hours later, Austin found himself knocking on the door of a first floor flat in a secluded building in St Johns Wood. A mere two blocks from his home on Abbey Road with its famed Beatles crosswalk and elegant mansion-houses, this building felt modern and rather drab. The small sign on the door read Dr Nicole Chinook. A thin, small woman in her mid-fifties with thick, Sally Jessy Raphael-style glasses let him in. As Austin stepped through the entryway and walked down the narrow hall, he noticed several hardbound novels and assorted baubles lining the bookshelves of the psychologist's home-turned-office. Christmas cards and theatre programmes were propped-up in front of rows of books. Degree certificates from various institutions hung on the walls. Austin began to imagine he was in a daytime television series with a certain Dr Nicole as the presenter. He was apprehensive but moreover he was angry with Zara for recommending this kook — his mother's favourite Americanism — instead of a legitimate therapist. He felt psychotic. Was he dreaming?

Inside the reception room, he saw half a dozen or more people. Among them a woman who bore a striking resemblance to Amanda Seyfried, complete with sea foam-coloured eyes, and a twenty-something with a military buzzcut and muscly arms that were disproportionate to his small head. They all watched him.

He woke up in a hospital bed ninety minutes later.

'It's perfectly natural,' said the attending doctor.

'What is?' Austin asked.

'It's trauma — traumatic what you've been through and how you reacted.'

Austin's body snapped upright in the gurney. 'But how do you know about that?' He said, not with anger but rather with curiosity. Momentarily, he believed the anger had been knocked out of him when his head hit the wooden floors of the psychologist's office.

'I told him.' Zara's voice and then, a few moments later, her body appeared from behind the curtains cordoning off Austin's hospital bed from the rest of the ward. 'Dr Chinook phoned me after she rang the ambulance. You gave us all a fright, Aus.'

That afternoon, Austin went for a series of CT scans and blood work. As time passed, his mind lacked the ability to form complex thoughts and sentence structures. For that, he felt relieved. He had grown tired of thinking. Tired of seeing things that were not there. Tired of trying to figure out where he had screwed, quite literally, up.

The hospital kept Austin overnight for observation. His deep sleep turned to vivid dreaming, impressions of which he recorded in his journal.

He looks the way I have always avoided — rugged and ethereal, his fitted cap tilted to the side of his head, his body thick with pheromones. He undresses slowly but leaves his ball cap and trainers on. I long to see the girth of his dick flop over the gentle crest of his balls as I fuck him from behind. And when I give it him, he moans so loudly I put my hand over his mouth to silence him. My flesh is all that is on his mind and he comes so quickly that I shoot my load inside of him without pulling out. And suddenly he's inside of me, pounding my ass so hard I think I might faint. I touch the viscous hair on his chest and whirl my tongue around his nipples. He bellows out that he wants more.

Six hours later, his eyes suddenly opened, then closed, then opened again, tears and sweat dripping down onto the flat pillow of the hospital bed where Austin lay motionless. He pushed aside the pillow and turned onto his stomach. His feet hung off the end of the bed, toes hooked over the edge.

What's wrong with me? he thought. That arse-hole gave me a disease and now I'm dreaming of sleeping with him? What the absolute fuck!

Comfort was the simple answer to what he was missing. It is an odd sensation to want comfort so bad that you yearn for someone that has hurt you in deep and unchangeable ways. Moments later, Austin fell back to sleep.

They drift against each other now. Sex is the lifeboat; sleep is the sea with a giant iceberg up ahead. As his breathing became irregular and his heartbeat quickened, Austin's muscles began to jerk. He's in deep sleep as he runs his fingers up Noah's thighs.

He was awake again in ninety minutes, still reeling from the dream, a sensation of being sucked down a vortex. As he fought between disillusionment and antagonism, he fumbled for his mobile phone to check the time. Even from a distance, he sensed his mother nearby. Scientists say infants are guided to their mothers' milk by their noses. Tiny glands on the breasts produce a fluid with a scent that attracts the baby. Austin never lost this sixth-sense. This is because, his mother once told him, everyone and everything has a vibrational energy signature. The closer someone is to you, the stronger that person's energy. But then again, she was kooky like that.

But not more than forty-five seconds later, she walked through the door of his hospital room with her hands clasped over her head, shoulders slumped as though she hadn't slept in days.

'You look like you need this bed more than I do, mum.' Austin looked at the matt of hair on top of her head, badly in need of a wash.

'And hello to you, Austin,' she replied tucking in her chin. 'How could you do this to me? I've been up all night worried, pacing the hallways of this god-forsaken NHS hospital' — The way she said NHS made Austin roll his eyes. — 'drinking poor vending machine coffee and wondering when you'd wake up to tell me the real story.'

She was the last person he wanted to deal with right now. Her latest round of advice and attempts at comfort had both only been trouble.

'Woah, woah, mum, cool it.' Austin bit his upper lip trying to hold back the urge to jump out of the bed, detaching IV needles and all, to leap at his mother's throat. 'How the hell did you even know I was in here?' And then he remembered. She was his emergency contact. Had been since he was sixteen and old enough to start seeing the GP on his own. He'd never bothered to update the record.

'You always said the NHS was one of the great things about living in Britain, mum. America could take a lesson from this country providing free healthcare. That's what you always say.'

'Yea well that's easy to say when your son, your only son, isn't stuck here hanging on for dear life.'

It took some moments for Austin to explain to her that (1) he wasn't dying (well, not in the way she'd made out), and (2) he had just fallen and bumped his head at the office. He used that phrase 'the office' to be vague about where he'd been before the ambulance ride. Only three days had passed since the diagnosis and no one knew except Zara. Not his work colleagues, not any other friends, and certainly not his mother.

'Save the prevarications for Oprah.' — Before, Austin would have been enraptured she knew a word like 'prevarication,' but right now he couldn't have cared less. — 'I know you were at a psychologist. Your girlfriend Zara told me.'

'Mother are you completely delusional?! I literally saw you not a week ago to tell you about Noah and how we broke up. You know I'm gay. You've met Zara a half dozen times at least, always as a friend, just a friend.' — He began to lose it now. — 'And where does she get off telling you that I was at a shrink's office when it happened? I'm thirty-four years old. For Christ's sake. I can take care of myself.'

'Well evidently you can't ... and anyway, she didn't tell me *why* you were there. Don't forget that I also told you to talk to someone, to get some help to get over what's his name ... the Jihadist.'

Austin snapped. 'GET THE FUCK OUT OF MY ROOM.'

She came back two hours later, looking more put-together. Her hair had been done and she walked with her chin level to the ground. She had also stopped at the hospital gift shop and bought a pre-packaged dozen of mixed carnations, irises, and daffodils with a smiley-face card tacked to the side of the vase.

'Before you say anything,' she began, 'I got you these.' She placed the vase on a table.

'Is that your way of saying you're sorry?' Austin always had to prod his mother to admit any sort of deep emotion, especially one that would make her appear vulnerable.

'Well anyway,' she said ignoring him, 'I thought the arrangement was nice.'

Nope, never could admit she was wrong, he thought, as she sat on the edge of his hospital bed.

'I saw Zara in the corridor earlier. She said all this has got to do with that boy —'

'Noah. His name is Noah.'

'— yea, him. That it's all got to do with him. You mind explaining that to me? Because God help me if he hurt you ...'. Her voice trailed off. She couldn't actually fathom what she might do if it turned out that Noah had in fact hurt her son.

'Well I suppose it does and it doesn't,' Austin said.

'Don't play coy with me, young man.'

'I'm not, I just don't know how to start.' He yanked at the intravenous tubes in his arms. He felt very small in the bed looking up at his mother. Having adjusted the cords enough, he sat upright but kept his eyes on the tubing. 'I've got HIV, mum.' This was the first time he said those words out loud. He thought saying it might make the clouds burst into a thunder storm and make the earth shake from its core. Instead, all that happened was that his mouth suddenly became very dry. He made to reach for a cup of water when his mother put her hand over his.

'That bastard gave it to you,' she said, not as a question but empathetically that she knew it to be true as sure as she knew her own name.

For once, Austin did not talk back to her nor try to correct her choice of language. Bastard had a certain ring to it.

Like the mother of a serial killer, Austin's mother was, of course, the last to recognise what her own son planned next. Reaching for the telephone on the adjustable table next to his hospital bed, Austin rang for the nurses' station.

'I'd like to see the hospital counsellor,' he said to the charge nurse. 'And I want my mum — my next of kin — to come along.' More than professional help, more than a way to deal with his emotions, Austin wanted his mother.

'It's an unusual request,' said Michael Waldron as Austin and Millicent sat before him. 'I see patients alone, always.' — He made to correct himself. — 'I suppose, most of the time.'

'I need moral support,' Austin said. The meekness in his voice cut through the sterility of the counsellor's room.

'And I know best as his mother.' — At this, the counsellor shot her a look. — 'And anyway,' she added, 'I don't believe in the talking cure. Spilling your guts, opening your heart to a stranger, and for what? To just have him look at you funny and scribble down notes.'

Both Austin and Waldron now gave her one of those looks.

'In my day,' she said, 'we got on with it; picked up the pieces of whatever drama we were going through and carried on. Keep calm and carry on, like the British say.'

'Look here, ma'am,' Michael Waldron said, 'I reckon we are about the same age, so I'm also from your day.'

'Hmphh,' she groaned.

'Austin let's focus on you. After all, you are why we are here. Now why do you think you re-acted as you did in the psychologist's office? Was it panic? If so, I can certainly understand. You've been through a lot in the last few days.'

'Well I don't understand it,' Austin's mother said. 'Maybe if he called me first, I could have helped him out.'

Haughtiness of her kind was not new to the hospital counsellor. 'I am addressing your son,' he said as she rolled her eyes. 'Go on, Austin.'

He spoke now: 'My chest felt tight; I pictured all these people staring at me, judging me with their eyes. I don't think it was real. I mean it seemed like a dream, but I passed out and then the next thing I remember is waking up here in hospital.'

'Hmphh,' his mother moaned again.

'And as for you, mum, I didn't call you because it didn't occur to me I should. I-I just had to take one thing at a time.'

'Couldn't call your own mother?! What an un-grateful child.' She said this to the room more than to anyone in particular.

The counsellor stepped in: 'When children have to act like parents, it affects them for life.'

Austin's mother flew out of her chair and grabbed Waldron by the shirt collar. 'I've been a good parent! Hell, I'm a great mother,' she screamed as the counsellor shoved her back down into her seat. 'Yea well,' she continued a few moments later as if never leaving the chair, 'It's not my fault he got AIDS.'

Curling his legs into his chest, Austin began to weep. She's some kind of manic, he thought.

She kept talking: 'He's always been reckless. Even as a kid. And look where it got him. An ungrateful man dying in front of me.'

'You need to leave, ma'am,' Michael Waldron said.

She snatched up her faded knockoff leather bag and stormed out of the room.

Austin's longing to be coddled by someone with a motherly instinct fell away. 'It was a mistake to ask her here,' he said. 'I want her dead.'

The counsellor had heard this before. Tortured individuals trapped in various forms of emotional abuse, often stemming from soured relationships with ex-lovers or difficult childhoods, made this statement many times in his office. Feelings of loathing are the result of years of emotional abuse. And yet he couldn't help, despite the dictums of professional distance, feeling sorry for this young man now in his office whom he imagined was being made to feel guilty for contracting HIV.

'I want to ask you a question, Austin. I'm guessing your mum has you on a bit of a rollercoaster, and probably always has done. Am I right?' His voice was kind.

Just then Austin could see himself as a nine-year-old boy. He'd woken up one morning before school to find his mother waiting in the loo with a toothbrush and a can of Ajax. 'Your teeth are ugly,' she said. He had needed to see a dental hygienist for some time, but she refused to take him. 'There's no petrol in the car and I'll be damned if I'm taking the bus' was invariably her excuse. He'd come home in tears two days before because one of the children on the school bus made fun of him, chanting 'yellow teeth, yellow teeth, yellow teeth' over and over. But even at age nine, Austin knew that Ajax was not for brushing one's teeth. He'd seen his nan use it to remove stains from pots and pans. 'Mummy, I can't put that in my mouth. It's for dirty dishes.' 'Rubbish,' she'd said. 'Ann Lancaster says it cleans like a white tornado. If it's good enough for Ann then it sure as hell is good enough for you, young man.' He tried not to swallow any of the Ajax as he brushed his teeth that morning.

'Sometimes having a traumatic childhood can cause a person to act out later in life by engaging in risky sexual behaviour,' Waldron said then.

'Surviving my childhood was a full-time job. And no, I haven't always been responsible, I've messed around and gotten myself into trouble here and there. But this, this disease is not because of her. I will not let her have this! It's because of him, because of Noah. I trusted him. I loved him.'

That night, for the first time since he met Noah, Austin's dream of the tsunami of fire recurred.

TWO

Dear, though the night is gone,
Its dream still haunts today ...

— W. H. AUDEN

Winter left London abruptly. The sky passed from a misty grey to a hazy blue-yellow. The soil smelled fresh with dew. Flesh-coloured tulips sprung up in Regent's Park. It felt like a genesis, of birthing what's new in life and clearing out the old in your space.

Sun rays were beating hard into the kitchen as Zara finished the washing up. She went over to the tiny French doors which opened onto a sub-urban balcony. It's odd, she thought, to call it a Juliet balcony. Juliet was Veronese, the doors are French, the house was Regency. Pulling the doors inwards, she turned to the front room, separated as it was from the kitchen-diner by only half of a wall.

'Austin, what *are* you doing?'

Is it unusual, then, to be sat on the sofa reading Monocle magazine on the first sun-filled Sunday of the year? He'd been quite content there for the better part of the morning, flicking through pages of the latest style and tech trends. It felt good to sit still, not thinking about his next doctor's appointment or the office or ...

'Austin — *hello*? Do you hear me?'

He looked up. 'Oh, good morning Zara.'

'What are you doing?' she asked again.

'Hmm, nothing much. Reading, trying not to think about anything in particular.'

Zara gawked at Austin and threw a dishtowel in his direction. It landed midway between his lap and the magazine held in both hands.

'You live in this house now. You need to help with the tidying up.' She had a nasty tone to her, the result of a bad night's sleep and growing frustration with her new roommate.

He swatted the dishrag off his boxer shorts and slapped the magazine down on the coffee table.

'I don't live here.'

'Let's see. You've been here' — she counted on her fingers — 'nine nights already.'

This infuriated Austin. He'd been living alone since the age of eighteen. He paid his own rent.

'That's sooo gracious, thank you.'

Zara walked over to the sofa and sat down. She positioned a throw pillow in the cushion crevices, effectively blocking her view of the visible slit in Austin's boxers.

'Look, that's the deal. You don't pay rent here,' she said, getting down to the fundamentals. 'When I asked you if wanted to recoup here —'

'Exactly. *You* asked.'

Though his words were sharp, he looked wounded. The unpleasantness she felt only a few moments ago disappeared. She repositioned the cushion and put her arm around his shoulders.

'Darling,' she said, 'I think it may be time for you to go. You're better now. You've got your routine with the meds, you just have to keep to the schedule, like the doctor said.'

Austin flopped forward on the sofa and stared at the uneven floor-boarding.

'Do you think so?'

'Mmm. I know you don't want to hear this. It's cliché, I know, but you can live an absolutely normal life now. Just like they say.'

He looked up at her. He struggled to find a sensible response to the statistic-laden dribble that fell from her cakehole.

'I'm sure the physicality of it all will be fine,' he said finally.

'What?' Zara said, innocent of the charge he silently placed on her. 'You can live a full and happy life, Austin. I'm not making this up.' She stood up again and returned to the balcony doors. 'I just don't know what's wrong with you these days.' She breathed in a waft of fresh air as she opened them. 'Actually, I do know. I think you're not over Noah —'

Austin stood up, about to protest.

'— Just do me a favour,' she went on anyway. 'Just confront him. Ask him why he did it. Maybe it will help.'

Austin sat down at the sofa table and crossed his legs Indian style. He could hear Zara walk to the other end of the flat and turn on the tap in the bathroom. As he took another breath, he closed his eyes, trying to bamboozle himself into happier thoughts, but things came off so convoluted. He struggled to see how speaking to Noah would make any difference. Closure was a word people threw around too much. It meant finality, a letting go of what once was, but he could not ever let go of the disease. He reached up and put both palms over his eyelids. He could sense his pupils straining under the weight of his sweaty fingers. He let his mind drift into the black, and it got darker and darker until it wasn't black at all but a warm, vibrant, intense auburn that reminded him of the glare of Noah's skin in the sunlight. His eyes opened reluctantly.

'I won't be here for lunch,' he called in Zara's direction.

He reached for his phone.

-- Meet at 2? The pub?

True to form, Austin arrived five minutes ahead of schedule. The pub sat empty, if you didn't count the odd assortment of stuffed toys hanging from the ceiling or the 1990s-era porn playing on old box-set televisions affixed to the countertops. He sat at one of the stools. The greasy hot scent of fried potatoes and crispy fish cooked on the hotplate behind the bar fanned through the air. Fine, it's all fine, he thought. This had to be dealt with on terms Noah could understand.

The bartender slid a Peroni across the counter, somehow managing to avoid the TV set and copious stacks of promo leaflets. Austin held the bottle to his lips. His way of drinking a beer was the same way people took liquid through a straw: gradually, deliberately, and in short bursts. He managed to down only three slurps by the time Noah walked through the door.

Noah looked the same — tussled hair, manicured beard, oversized jeans and hoodie — but there was something off about his demeanour. The eyes moved too much, blinking like he wore new contacts that hadn't yet settled in. His hands quavered as he stuck out the right one to greet Austin.

'Sit down,' Austin said, feeling superior. 'We need to talk.'

Noah obliged and nodded to the bartender. Soon his own Peroni was slung across the bar.

'What's good?'

'What's ... good ...?' Austin's mood shifted to exasperation. 'Is that some Americanism you picked up from one of your hipster friends?'

Noah sat stone-faced and chugged at his beer.

'It just means "you alright?" ... okay?'

'I know what it means.'

Austin clasped his hands and pressed them together tightly to regain his composure. This was his chance. He needed to know why. 'Why' wasn't the question, in effect. It was more like 'how' or 'when' or maybe it was all of those wrapped into one.

Sure the bartender was at a safe distance away, Austin steeled himself and stared Noah in the eyes. 'Listen, I have HIV.'

He said this flatly and in saying it expected a reaction full of heavy shame, full of guilt weighing down on the listener's shoulders. To accompany this expectation, Austin did something he hadn't done in weeks: he allowed himself a tiny bit of empathy for Noah.

'No! Really?' Noah said, shaking his head furiously and then picking up his Peroni to finish it off. 'Oh. My. God. Are you okay now? I mean what happened?' His voice had a roughness to it that was eased only by the Hollywoodised accent he seemed to be adopting. His prerogative put deeper edges around the words.

'Are you fucking serious?' Austin clinched his fists underneath the lip of the bar. He was at a loss over what to do with the rest of his body. Every other piece of it was limp and betrayed. 'Don't play this game with me. You gave it to me.' His voice grew louder.

Neither of them noticed the bartender approach to offer second rounds. Noah looked to the floor and shook his head again, more vigorously this time.

'I see,' he said finally and motioned for another beer but turned back to the floor. 'Is there somewhere else we could talk? Proper, like?'

A ten-pound note got tossed across the bar. 'Around the corner, now,' said Austin leaning into his advantage.

The alleyway behind the pub was lit by a single overhead bulb of the type used to keep insects at bay. Austin stood with the light overhead. This was a trick he used with hostile witnesses. Placing the light on oneself put the other at physical ease and therefore more likely to open up.

'Just tell me one thing,' he said staring into the shadowy outline that was Noah. 'Why didn't you tell me you had it? I would have understood.'

His distress was obvious and for a moment Noah considered matching it with his own distressed rendition of the old *you say that now* line. Instead, he grew harder.

'I don't know what you're on about, mate.' His regular East London accent returned.

'What! What! What?' Austin murmured, each iteration a bit more fearful. He began to feel like a whale in shallow water.

'Nothing, okay? Nothing!' Noah stepped closer and the frontal regions of his face grew clearer with the light.

'All I ever asked was for you to be honest with me.' At once, Austin's bafflement turned to anger. 'To tell the truth. That's a basic requirement for a relationship.'

'Well let's talk about it then.'

'Who did you sleep with?'

'Bloody hell, you think you're dench now? Like you in some position of authority or something?'

'Don't be so awfully working class, Noah.' This had become ideological in Austin's mind. 'I've been to your family home. I've seen where you come from.'

'Oh. I'm. So. Sorry.' The Valley Girl inspired accent returned. 'You *ingratiated* your way into my life and now you wanna know who I've been fucking with?' He stepped closer still. 'Big enough word for you?'

'This is pointless,' Austin said, 'I'm going now.'

Noah pushed him on the shoulder, knocking him back a step. 'I can't even tell you.'

'Tell me what? What!?'

'Too many to name. But yea the last one was the Muslim chick I told you about already. I never tried to hide it.'

This was true, on the surface. Austin was not averse, in truly painful times, to crying, to kicking, to screaming, to doing whatever it took to release a drop from the emotional wellspring constantly bubbling beneath the surface of his ribcage. But he wouldn't allow Noah the satisfaction of seeing him break down.

He leaned forward so his face lurked a mere few inches from Noah's. 'I don't know why I'm surprised. Should never have gotten mixed up with someone like you.'

He practised this line on Zara but saying it now to its intended recipient was liberating. With his body twisted out of shape and his eyes aflame with fury, Austin ran off.

Hannah Lamott-Wilhoit was twelve years old when she was sent off to a boarding school in Montreux. She was not the only girl from England in her class of twenty-five, but she was the only one from the sleepy Home Counties suburb of Stevenage. The vast majority of the other new students in her year were from Paris or Brussels or Hong Kong or any of the array of cities the upper-middle-class families of gifted or otherwise rich children inhabit. Hannah, by virtue of circumstance, was one of the gifted ones. She did well in maths, excelled in the limited science subjects the local primary school taught, and she used vocabulary far exceeding the playground-basic lexicon of other year sixes. What Hannah's two fathers lacked in financial resources, they made up for with ingenuity. So, when she scored impressively on the eleven-plus examination, Nick (aka Dad) convinced Jamal (aka Papa) to scour the internet in search of private school scholarships.

The summer before Hannah left for Switzerland, she spent nine of her fifteen waking hours every day immersed in books. While other children were playing Xbox, going to the cinema, or hanging out at the local lido, Hannah read biographies of political leaders, compendiums of world history, and novels by Lois Lowry and Murakami, but mostly by Zadie Smith. She loved Smith and although it was discussed in hush tones by Jamal and Nick, no one had the heart to tell her that the curriculum at Montreux Boarding was unlikely to include Zadie. Not that this bit of information would have made any difference to Hannah. She liked what she liked, and the things she liked were generally two or three or ten years beyond her age bracket.

In some ways, then, it shouldn't have come as a shock when Hannah did what she did. Little girls with big ideas need access to material which will fuel their creativity, and when they don't have that access, they'll go to great lengths to acquire it.

Stealing a library book was tough business in Montreux. At first the librarians thought little Hannah forgot to return the book on time (Maybe they don't have the same courtesy for property where *she* comes from?), but when six weeks passed and Hannah still clung onto her copy of Smith's *On Beauty*, the teachers got involved, and then the headmistress, until finally at three months and four days, Nick was rang. 'Bonjour, monsieur ... Your - err - daughter refuses to return the book ... It's beyond her reading comprehension ... We really don't understand ... You'll have a word with her then?' But Hannah categorically refused, even after Jamal intervened to say he would buy her a copy of the damned book just to put a stop to this whole ridiculous mess. Nothing doing. She wanted this book, *this* copy, complete with its dog-eared pages and underlines and highlights in three different ink colours thanks to unseen upperclassmen. It was a window into a world in which Hannah knew she belonged, a world where mental capacity meant boundless opportunity. Four-hundred-and-forty-three pages away from Stevenage.

In short, Hannah got expelled from Montreux weeks before the end of her first term there. Such obstinate children were not welcome. She was allowed to keep the book, but only after Nick paid

15.25 Swiss Francs in late charges. Jamal very unhelpfully pointed out that a new copy of Zadie Smith's masterpiece would have only cost about nine pounds.

'She's fine now,' Nick said looking around at the group, 'we got her into one of the independent schools in Hitchin.'

Everyone clapped.

'It's your turn now, Austin,' said Michael Waldron, nodding first and then looking down onto his yellow notepad.

From his vantage point at one end of the semicircle of chairs, Austin could survey the faces of all nine other attendees. This simultaneously shattered and enhanced his confidence. He looked around once more, hoping to latch onto a pair of sympathetic eyes. Everyone looked down, afraid to get too personal.

'Can I take a pass this week?'

Biscuits and tea are the after-hours staple of all good (and most bad) support groups. Once his Earl Grey had been doused with sufficient long-life milk, Austin stood at the corner of the room and attempted to balance the paper cup on the outstretched palm of one hand whilst eating a shortbread with the other.

'Need some help there?'

'Oh, hello,' Austin said, placing the biscuit on top of the paper cup and extending his right hand. 'It's Nick, isn't it?'

The cup jiggled precariously, but Austin paid it no mind. Nick's hand was warm and dry to the touch, and this small wonder spoke volumes when compared against the sweaty, moist hands of the other group attendees that greeted Austin that evening.

'And you're Austin. First time here?'

Nick smiled, a smile so magazine-quality perfect that Austin blushed. He had the idea this was how A-list celebrities were meant to look: *So different to normal people, and yet *so* alike one another.* Hundreds or thousands of such people exist in Hollywood and maybe a dozen or so live in places like Manhattan or the sixteenth arrondissement of Paris, but no one thought — until then — that they lived in Stevenage and came to group in Kings Cross.

'It is, yes. I was just diagnosed,' Austin grabbed on tighter to his Earl Grey, 'and by "just" I mean a few weeks back.'

This was met with a sympathetic nod of Nick's angular jaw.

'And your partner — Jamal, is that what he's called? — he has HIV?'

'No, no. I'm not one of the freeloaders — people here only for "peer support" or whatever.'

He made inverted commas in the air, gave a hearty laugh, and shot out the toothiest smile yet. It was like Nick knew about his singularity and yet didn't take himself all that seriously.

Now freshly interested, Austin spoke louder. '*You* have HIV?'

'Yup.'

'So, do you have a lot of friends in this group?'

'Nope.'

'You don't know any of these people?'

'I know two or three — seen their faces week-after-week. I mean you do get that —'

Austin's head jerked. 'Right ...'

'— But it's hard to make meaningful connections at these things. People all have their own motivations, etcetera ...'. Nick looked worried. 'I can see I've lost you.'

'No, not at all,' Austin said, his voice thick with plea. Nick was the *essence* of lowkey celebrity in some way, not an outcast on the HIV support group circuit.

'What are you in for?'

This sort of prison-like humour had never done much for Austin, but it was somehow endearing on Nick.

'Michael was my counsellor in hospital, and he recommended the group ...' He added after some thought: '... I don't really know why I'm here.'

'I'd suppose you're here because, like me, you want a community.'

Swallowing the spit in the back of his throat, Austin tried to let go of his curious anxiety. 'That's it.'

'Hey, listen,' said the should-be-famous Nick, pulling out his mobile phone. 'Why don't we exchange numbers? It's good to have a buddy — keep each other informed about time changes or inclement weather or whatever — if you plan to come back, that is?'

'Yes, I will definitely be back.'

Austin felt a great tenderness well up inside when he received Nick's text inviting him to the birthday party. There was no name for this feeling. It was something like admiration and awe and partial disbelief. People didn't invite Austin places, other than Zara of course. Dramatic, life-changing circumstances tend to generate dramatic emotions and so Austin was careful not to appear too eager in accepting. Once. It had only been one meeting for one minute at one very odd support group.

Still, Austin could be certain this was friendship. For in one moment you are dying and in the next you are going to the party of a man you don't know.

Now, his once-buzzing brain froze. Standing in the doorway was the most handsome guy he had ever laid eyes on. Streaked-grey brown hair left just long enough to be stylish and a body only ever seen on film or in magazines. It figures, Austin thought, Nick would marry a guy like this. And that made two A-listers living in Stevenage. Together, naturally.

Jamal looked uneasily at his guest. He had an impulse to interrogate him, to find out everything there was to know about the mysterious friend his husband invited at the nth hour to a birthday party that had been months in the making.

'You alright?' he said, keeping his composure, and then, 'Come through. Nick's in the garden with the others.'

The lawn teemed full of people. Parties seemed larger and more rushed these days. Austin could remember his grandmother spending weeks, maybe months planning a birthday or an anniversary gathering. Now celebrations of that sort could happen at will. Hadn't Nick only organised this soiree three days ago? Or had Austin been a last-minute invite?

The birthday boy stood near a portico separating the interior from the patchy yard. Around him were a handful of professorial types.

'I guess I mean there should be a revolution of sorts, you understand, like the way the French had theirs ...' he was saying.

'Like the French?' a red-haired woman said, 'Surely more like the Americans!'

Feeling this was not his crowd, Austin began to walk in the direction of a drinks station setup on the opposite end of the concrete.

'Austin!' came the shout from Nick, 'I'm so chuffed you made it. Come, meet my friends.'

Introductions were swiftly made, and Austin got the suspicion that Nick bent the truth about people in ways that were exceedingly flattering. Amy with the red hair was apparently one of the top political scientists in all of not just the Southeast, but in Britain. Meg's family were made out to be billionaires with homes across Europe. Harry's father owned a conglomerate of successful something-or-another. Everyone blushed and beamed while concurrently doing their own version of *oh stop*. Suspicions were confirmed when Nick made to introduce Austin. 'And this is a dear friend, Austin, who I met at group. Austin is one of London's highest-paid criminal barristers.' This was not, unfortunately, true but like those gone before,

Austin grew flush and said, 'Oh do stop, Nick. You're embarrassing me.'

Jamal approached with a tray of champagne flutes. 'What's all this about?'

'Just introductions, babe.'

Nick reached for the tray and handed Austin a glass. Jamal passed flutes to the others.

'Let's have a toast then, shall we?' Everyone raised their glasses. 'To me, on my birthday!'

'Happy birthday, Nick,' Austin said and took a second gulp of bubbly.

'And now, if *I* may,' Jamal interjected, 'Happy birthday to my dear husband.'

Hannah poked her head out from behind a Nintendo Switch. 'Happy birthday, dad!'

Jamal moved in to kiss Nick, but Nick took a sip of champagne.

Austin noticed this roughness between them. He was uncertain as to what to do to disarm the cycle of friction his presence caused. Once begun, such cycles are hard to break; each phrase spoken, each look given all contribute to the kinetics of the thing.

Suddenly Nick and Austin are kissing. Again, and again until Austin thinks he'll never have enough. His head bent back taking it all in.

'Austin?' the voice calls, 'Austin?'

Austin opened his eyes. Nick was shaking him.

'Are you okay?'

He scratched his eyes with his palms. 'Oh I'm, I'm sorry. I must have dozed off there.'

Daydreaming is like remembering. It felt real. Or the feeling of it wanting to be real felt real. And that was enough. Jamal came closer now and pulled Nick away. Austin stood there surrounded by a trio of strangers whose identities had all been conflated like his own. Who were these people; what kind of life did Nick lead?

'So, as I was saying,' ginger Amy went on like nothing had happened, 'the French had it figured out when it came to revolutions. Chop off their heads and let them eat cake and all that.'

'Shouldn't we check on this friend of Nick's?' This was Harry speaking, and although Austin stood not more than a metre away, they spoke as though he were not there.

To be seen, I have to be invisible, Austin thought.

'Don't worry about me,' he spoke up, 'I'll be going.'

'I think,' said Jamal as he pulled his husband into the mud room off the portico, 'it would be a shame to ruin this day over someone you only just met.'

Nick grimaced. 'Did I do something wrong?'

'I'm glad to see *your* spirit hasn't been destroyed by it.'

Nick had it. Whatever it is: raw energy, charisma, hypnotic magnetism. He had it in spades. But he wasn't a believer in personal presentation, and this made it all more enviable and all the more powerful. Put another way, he never set out to seduce anyone, he went about seducing everyone; there's a big difference. For his part, Jamal knew this, but it did not excuse the situation at hand. Nor did the fact it was Nick's birthday. Monogamy knows no holiday.

'What are you talking about?' Nick asked in earnest.

Jamal turned to walk back outside. 'Nothing.' The reasons for simplification are often ideological.

'It's not nothing, Jay,' Nick said grabbing him by the shoulder. 'Too much with Austin?'

'It's like you don't realise when you are doing it. You're leading him on.'

'I'm just being myself,' Nick said, to be both clever and remote.

'Anybody can see the guy is lonely, he's probably torn up about his diagnosis. He needs a friend, not a love interest. *Especially* not a married one.'

This wasn't about trust, Nick got that. He'd never cheated and never would, but people live in their own echo chambers.

'I get it. I'll take care of it.' He leaned forward and gave Jamal a kiss.

Austin stood on the train platform and exhaled, catching off-guard a lady passing by with her dog. He felt guilty, but also immune. He wasn't in the business of breaking up relationships, but he also hadn't asked for Nick's overt displays of affection. On the train ride back, he closed his eyes and let his mind float.

At Kings Cross, the opening of the doors let in a thick smog to enliven Austin from his preoccupation. He hurried out of the station and called an Uber. On the twenty-one-minute ride, he recorded his daydreaming in his journal.

Although I can't be more than eight or nine years old, I recognise his face. He is scruffy around the edges, but his dark tightly-cut auburn hair and five-o'clock shadow are well maintained. He approaches me methodically and offers me a sweet, something like out of an after-school special where a mother tells her child to never take candy from a stranger. He's 19, maybe 20 years old and after I take the candy, he guides me into the passenger seat of his car.

We're cruising at 80 miles per hour down the motor-way when the lorry smashes into the right-hand side of the vehicle. Blood, visceral everywhere. The lifeless look on his face.

It was the second time that day he'd been carried away by false memories. What caused such dark thoughts?

A tall narrow mirror hung in the entryway to his flat. Stepping through the front door, Austin became aware, suddenly, of his own stomach and the way it had flattened considerably since his release from hospital. He ate more than ever now, but he had put on weight in the right places and his physique tightened in all the other spots. He'd been warned the medication could cause changes in appetite and weight fluctuation; he'd never imagined this particular side-effect would be one he appreciated. Austin put his right hand on his stomach to determine if the reflection was accurate, and finding it was, he moved his hand lower until he felt the elastic band of his briefs. He grew hard little-by-little and he moved his hand lower still and began jerking off vigorously until he came in a shower of white all over the mirror. He was aware of his own body and the desire for it for the first time since the diagnosis. It was amazing.

Noah Hakim was in a shit-load of trouble. His parents were fed-up; why was he now constantly short on money? What was he spending his salary on? And now that Asha had been caught last week smoking up at work, the supervisor wanted to see him. There were no coincidences. Noah knew that much. He put on a plain black t-shirt, a bit wrinkled but he wasn't in the mood for ironing, and without his mother to do his laundry, the available options of clean clothes dwindled. As he pulled on a pair of crumpled khaki trousers, it occurred to him momentarily it might be worth making things right with Lilly and Aashirbaad just to get his laundry done. It was a passing thought and after he did up his laces, he remembered his right — that's what it was, his absolute moral and legal right — to be independent, without interference from anyone: not his father, not his mother, and unequivocally not Austin.

Sat outside the supervisor's office of the Midwifery Council, the burn still lingered in Noah's nose from the cocaine he snorted only a few minutes before, but years of practice made him cautious about snorting too deeply in public. Normally this kind of burn could be alleviated with another quick sniff. He stood up to duck outside when the supervisor called for him. Shit.

It was all over in less than five minutes. Noah had little explanation. He didn't even realise the company searched employee lockers at random. He had a right to privacy, didn't he? And anyway, it's a sort-of hobby, not like it effects his work performance or anything. These excuses didn't land well and when the pink slip was handed over, Noah felt an odd sort of freedom. Until he got home and realised three tins of vegetables, four ramen packets, and two sachets of coke weren't going to last him very long with only a few pounds to his name.

Austin leaned back in the chair. His eyes were pink around the rims and blue-grey bags sat in the corners. It had been a hard night, but the finely-print leaflet in the bottle said this was normal. It took time to adjust to medication and a few nights of rough sleep were to be expected.

On the computer screen, a dozen emails popped up, and Austin sighed. His mind could not focus on work today. Instead he thought about the

Black Death, the great plague which wiped out half the population of the West. He envied those 14th century Europeans who caught the Yersinig pestis bacteria that ultimately killed them. They had each other. It was a populist disease after all, carried along the Silk Road and later passed from merchant to sailor on ships throughout the Mediterranean. Most victims died within seven days after initial infection, some in as little as two. Who has time to feel sorry for oneself in two days? But with this, with his disease, he had years, decades. Even the onset of AIDS is progressive, eventually allowing opportunistic infections and cancers to thrive. Austin didn't want to play host to any opportunistic thriving. He wanted what those Middle Ages Europeans had: a community.

Just then his phone buzzed. It was Nick.

-- I'm sorry about the party, bro, I should've been on better behaviour. X

-- Nick, I'm not sure what you mean ...

His fingers moved in rapid succession.

-- I'm the one that should be apologising. Wasn't trying to cause any fights between you and Jamal.

-- Don't be daft. I came on a bit too strong. Been known to do that. Didn't mean anything by it.

Austin sighed. He liked Nick, but not in any decidedly romantic way. Yes, there was that momentary fantasy of their kissing, but it was a one-off thing and he'd never let Nick know about it. In fact, he missed group counselling last week to avoid any awkwardness.

    -- Do you think we can be friends? It would be nice to share stuff with somebody in the same boat.

    -- Course we can! :) I need a good friend too. See you at group this week then?

    -- You bet. Xx

When Noah's time came, he stood at the front of the conference room and pulled at the back of his jeans, which fell due to not being affixed to a belt. Let's just get on with it, he thought. His hands were shaking, but he couldn't be sure if this was from nerves or given the forced withdrawal he had been enduring for forty-eight hours. Gaseousness filled his insides as though he might vomit.

It was a panel interview, and there was no one there to guide him through it. In fact, he hadn't heard the term 'panel interview' before three days ago when a Mr Monsanto from the Jobcentre called to ask if Noah would be interested in a janitorial job in Brixton at some sort of art gallery. He needed a job since he'd gotten fired from The Midwifery Council, so here he was about to wing his way through a panel interview. Brixton wasn't a bad place to be either, he thought, if you were interested in scoring something, which he was. And he liked art, this was good. That sort of thing ought to matter at a gallery, even for a cleaner.

The questions were straightforward, and it took Noah a few minutes to realise what this panel interview was about. He had thought it was a test. Instead, he understood it was a means of intimidation. If you could answer the questions — most of which were related to schooling, past employment, any relevant experience — and not buckle, you were in.

He cinched it. His references weren't stellar, but if anyone could defy the fates of employment, Noah felt it must be him. As he tied his shoelaces and prepared to walk out of the conference room, Noah turned to Mr Monsanto, who sat in the centre of the interviewers.

'And my favourite artist is Giotto.'

Getting a new job was an event for anyone in the extended Hakim family, but to say Noah thought Lilly and Aashirbaad would be thrilled at his new line of work would be a massive overstatement. But he told them anyway, his laundry still needing to be done and his refrigerator running perilously low. So, it was then over Sunday lunch that Lilly Hakim disapproved of Noah's new means of gainful employment almost as much as she disapproved of him being fired from his previous job. If there is one thing she liked less than her own dreams of a career having gone unfulfilled, it was seeing her eldest son so royally mess up his own prospects in life. For his part, Aashirbaad was just happy to know he wouldn't have to foot any of Noah's bills.

'Your eyes are red,' said Iman, the middle boy, between bites of mashed potato.

'Mind your own business, punk,' sneered Noah.

'Both of you stop,' said Lilly and then looking more closely at Noah added, 'You do look a bit tired, dear.'

'I'm fine —'

'Inshallah,' said Aashirbaad.

'— just tired. Hitting the streets looking for jobs is tough, eh?'

This was a side of her son Lilly never noticed. 'What is this "hitting the streets"? Since when do you use language like that?'

'Never mind,' said Aashirbaad, 'but stay well. You need to work. To provide for yourself.'

Noah raced out of his seat. 'Far be it from you to help out your own son.'

'Watch your mouth, young man, I am still your father.'

But it was too late, Noah got up and left the family house.

Austin's great talent as a lawyer was perseverance. Where his colleagues excelled at logic, analytical skills, and creativity, Austin had the resolve to complete the work necessary to drive a case to a successful finish. 'By any means necessary' became a sort-of professional mantra he stole from Sartre or Malcolm X, he couldn't remember which (he'd read both, of course). You might get an email from his clerk asking for something or another and moments later Austin himself would be at your desk asking for the very same thing. He took solicitors aside at sector-wide parties and persuaded them to send their clients his way. It worked not because he was the only one doing it, but because his skills in the area of false flattery and faked deference were far superior to anyone else's, thanks to having seen those abilities lived out in his mother all his life.

'I won't tell anyone,' Austin said, but whatever he was told invariably ended up being retold, either to this clerk or to Zara over weekend cocktails or to Nick in what became an almost continuous text conversation. It was a wonder, really, he could at all be considered a good lawyer, much less a sound criminal barrister, considering how he violated the attorney-client privilege on a regular basis. And yet, he had a way about him that engendered trust in his clients. They sensed he was one of them, not a criminal himself per se but someone in which criminals could place their trust.

'You see the thing is, Mister,' said the eighteen-year old with messy blonde hair and an oversized polo shirt, 'I did it.'

'You did what, Liam?' Austin always insisted on calling his clients by their first names. He thought it served to relax them.

'I did *it*.' Liam cocked one eyebrow.

Austin put his hands up. 'Oh no, let me stop you right there. I don't want to hear if you did or didn't commit the crime. Or rather how you did it. It's not my job to know.'

'Huh?' Liam said with surprise. 'Of course it's your job, you're my solicitor.'

'I'm your barrister, and it will not affect my defence of you whether you did it or not. I prefer to think you didn't, so I can go in there with a clear conscience.'

'But the thing is, Mister' — Liam tended to start all important sentences this way. — 'I don't have anyone to open up to you, you know.' (Austin did.) 'If you would just let me get some stuff off my chest, then I think it would help ... It would help me. I dunno if it will do anything for my defence or for you.'

On second thought, it could do a hell of a lot for me, Austin thought, to hear someone else's story for a while. He encouraged Liam to continue talking.

'I stole that money, you see, Mister. I went to that grocery store and I calmly asked the man at the till to hand over the cash the shop had on hand. Turned out to be a measly two hundred quid. I didn't even think it through proper like, ya know?'

Austin shook his head.

'Well I didn't put on no mask or try to hide myself from the security cameras or whatever. That's pretty dumb innit?'

'Why did you do it that way? You couldn't have thought you'd get away with it?'

Liam rolled his eyes. 'Well I weren't thinking of that when I did it, was I?' — Austin stared at him. — 'My only goal was to feed myself and get some place to stay for a month or somethin' til I could get back on my feet.'

This was new information to Austin. 'You're homeless?' Liam's clothes were clean, he appeared well-shaven, and despite his south-of-the-river accent, he seemed in Austin's mind to be rather well-spoken; at least more sympathetic than the majority of his clients, most of whom were accused of grievous bodily harm or worse, not a petty theft charge.

'Were,' said Liam, 'I *were* homeless, but I got myself sorted since then. Got a little studio flat down south, proper home ya know ... Bloody English legal system takes ages to process crimes like mine.'

'I don't know what it is like to be homeless, Liam,' Austin said. Liam's face carried an expression of yea, no shit on it. 'But did you try some other methods before resorting to theft?'

'Yea I did all the tricks, Mister. I begged for money. Shit, I even rode the tube going from person to person asking for change. But the thing is that nobody sees homeless guys ... I mean they see you enough to walk to the other side of the street or to look down instead of lookin' into your eyes.'

'You felt like you were out of options?'

'Yea I guess I did. I weren't really thinking anymore at that point.'

'How did you feel afterwards? What did you do with the two-hundred pounds?'

'After that ... what I did ... I felt like nothing were real. I went to a hostel, one of those real cheap ones round Piccadilly where loads of kids stay when they ain't got no money but want to visit the big city ... It was' — and this was new to him, the first time he thought it through — 'like I was free of the streets but locked up even more inside my mind. I sunk so low that I stole from innocent people. That shit hurt me. I even felt guilty takin' a shower in the hostel. Felt nice bein' clean and all but I knew I didn't do nothing to deserve it. I done worse than stealin', Mister, I killed myself on the inside, only I didn't know it then. And all this, everything that's happened since, it goes to show that I shouldn't have done it in the first place, cause everything worked out in the end anyway.'

For a moment Austin envied this young man sat in front of him. Though Liam no doubt earned a fraction of the salary Austin made, and though Austin had certainly been given more opportunities in life than this boy ever had, he sensed Liam found something he hadn't: inner peace. A great sense of loneliness and isolation washed over Austin.

'Why'd you end up on the streets in the first place?' Austin asked, leaning into this client.

'Well I'm gay, ain't I?'

Dumbfounded, Austin didn't say a word. Liam was what Austin and Zara referred to as 'trade': someone you would never identify as anything other than straight.

Liam continued: 'Well when they found out, my mum and pops kicked me out the house.'

'That's awful,' said Austin. 'It must be horrible to go through, especially at your age.'

'Oh for fuck's sake, Mister. I know you're gay too, bruv.'

'Oh?' Austin avoided saying more.

'You ain't that obvious-kinda-fag, but I got good gaydar. ... But as I was sayin' ... when the coppers locked me up, they done me a favour, cause that's when the homeless agency got in touch and helped me get on benefits and get my flat from the council ... then when I had my flat, I got a job.'

Austin had never heard one of his clients say they were grateful for having been arrested.

'It's easier to get a job when you got an address to list on the application form,' Liam said as if teaching Austin a life lesson (and maybe in some way he was), 'and well I know now I gotta face some penalty for what I did but least I turned my life round.'

Returning to his desk, Austin picked up his iPhone.

'Hey Z., got a minute? ... Am I the only one who still feels like a child?'

'I think we all do,' answered Zara from the end of the other line. 'What's this all about?'

'I've got this new client, you see. He's a working-class kid, teenager. I took on his case pro bono through the agency.'

Austin told her about Liam. Zara could sense in his tone he had been moved by the boy's plight.

'That's a sad story. Kinda makes you think about what you have, huh?'

'Not only that,' said Austin, 'but I feel for him.' He sat silent for a moment. 'I mean I feel sorry for him, and I want to help him, but I can't stop thinking that he's somehow helping me.'

'Go on,' Zara said, biting down a smile.

'It's just that, well I think, I'm not so bad off.'

'You've been through a lot ...'

'Not like this kid. I'm not trying to downplay what I've gone through. Yea, it's hell. I can't even say "gone through" — that's like saying it's over and done — but I just felt like a child with him there in my office schooling me on what it means to be an adult and to deal with your shit.'

'And what about that support group, are you still going?'

'Yea, I mean, I think I want to go back.' — He thought of Nick then. — 'But it can get depressing, though. Everyone on about their problems.'

'But that's what you do for a living. You help people solve problems ... Maybe the group could help you solve your own.'

It's all so bloody lame, to be cleaning up after rich, white people who come to poor, black Brixton to see art by middle-class imitators. And he felt sick, on all levels: physical and mental and emotional. I need to get well, Jesus Christ, I need to get well. He kept repeating these words to himself, invoking a god he neither revered nor believed in. He put the mop he was holding into a bucket full of soiled water and licked the end of his finger. Reaching into the pocket of his coveralls, the subtleness of the wet finger made contact with the white powder. He moved the finger up to his nose, taking time to observe the shape and texture of the drug on its ascent. He no longer cared if anyone saw. The drugs no longer worked anyway. A temporary high cannot decrease chronic guilt.

Hot. Burning hot. Cold. Icy cold. He experienced these two extremes end-on-end. And then hot, hotter, even hotter. He will vomit for sure now. Dizzy. The room is spinning. And then black. Everything is a shadowy black. He should sit down. But the voices ramble incessantly. And then his hearing has faded. And he collapsed.

Mr Monsanto was standing over him when he came to. The mop and bucket were at rest near his head. He blinked rapidly and then tried to remember which day it was. He wanted to speak, perhaps to ask Monsanto how long he had been lying there, but when he went to open his mouth, it itched with a dryness like dandruff stuck to his tongue. His lips too tingled as if they had fallen asleep. Pins and needles shot up the sides of his face. And then he saw Monsanto's mouth move. Attached to long, skinny arms, Monsanto held out a small plastic bag.

Noah tapped on his right ear. The sound of a prickle grew faint. He tapped on the left ear. The prickle became louder. At last, Monsanto's voice was audible.

'Noah, Noah, Noah.' Repeating someone's name over again and again was the only thing Monsanto could think to do when he found his employee passed out in the centre of the main exhibition space. He'd stopped this nominal repetition only once in the past three minutes, and that was when he noticed a small package containing a powdery substance had fallen out of Noah's pocket.

'Noah, Noah, Noah.'

Noah managed to sit up now, and his butt began to ache as he repositioned himself on the floor. Monsanto stopped his chanting as suddenly as he began it.

'You listen to me, now, Noah, listen to me ...'

Noah stared. What choice did he have but to accept the inevitability of losing another job?

'... I can help you get help.'

'What are you talkin' about?' Noah's mouth spewed dust particles as he spoke.

Monsanto reached his free hand over to Noah and pulled him to his feet. The other hand still held the precarious dime bag which he jiggled sideways.

'Do you think I don't notice what's going on?'

'So, I'm done for then?'

'No, I said I can help you. I will get you help, Noah.'

Looking at his boss, Noah saw everything he hated about authority, about relationships, about life in fact. His well-tailored suit, his refined Queen's English, his limp wrist reeking of class.

Noah hated all of it. It all came down to the want or need of other people to control his life for their own ends.

'You don't know shit about drugs, 'cept maybe your rich daddy's friends let you try some when you were at uni or some shit.' Noah couldn't grasp his vibrating pulse. He inhaled a few short breaths to calm himself.

'People have different experiences with addiction. Do you think you're the only one?'

Noah knew he wasn't the only one, and each person has a 'completely different process' — he'd read that in some internet blog somewhere. But he did not want help. He wanted to get rid of his guilt. He had released the poison into Austin's veins. No one else had to suffer on his account. He just wanted to be well. But Monsanto was still talking.

'... People are cut from the same cloth. I'm a recovering addict, I can help.'

Noah stood up and steadied himself.

'Fuck off. I don't want your help.'

He tore the bag out of Monsanto's hand and raced toward the exit.

'Memory is a strategy,' said Michael Waldron as he looked around the semicircle. 'If you can recall the forgotten or the suppressed, you can put these memories to work for you.'

Tina, the mother of a girl who contracted HIV at fourteen from a blood transfusion, stuck her hand in air, 'I don't think I really get it.'

'It's okay,' Waldron's voice was kind; he'd been doing this awhile. 'What I mean to say is that history, memory, and narrative are all tied up. We're all haunted by something.'

'That's the truth,' Tina said, nodding with comprehension.

'I wondered if someone else would like to speak now.' He looked around again. 'Austin, why don't you go?'

Austin knew his day was coming. Everybody who goes to group knows they will have to speak, but each session you get away with silence feels like a little victory and you soon start thinking maybe you'll be the one that never has to step up to the proverbial podium. He sighed.

'Hello, hi, my name is Austin. I have HIV.' From his breast-pocket he pulled out a piece of paper folded in ten ways. 'I prepared some notes, if that's —'

'Let's not rely on prepared statements, okay?' said Waldron using a phrase familiar to Austin.

He crumpled the paper and stuck it back in the pocket. 'Yes, okay then. Right. Well ...'

Telling someone like Austin to put away their notes was akin to taking away their crutches. He hobbled for a while on the right words. When the right words never came, he decided using the wrong ones would just have to do.

'... Six weeks ago, I tested positive. I am a privileged white man who grew up in "good neighbourhoods." I never stuck a needle in my arm, nor am I a sex worker. I slept with men — only one actually, the one who gave it to me — and we didn't use protection and I got HIV. That's it. That's the whole back story.'

Austin looked around the room. Tina looked bored. Other attendees were scribbling on notepads or twiddling their thumbs. Only Nick seemed to be silently shouting words of encouragement. After several seconds, Michael Waldron looked up.

'I think we want to hear more, Austin. Tell us your story.'

No one looked like they wanted more, but Austin let out a moan of anxiety and continued anyway.

'I'm struggling quite a lot with definitions, you know?' — This caught Tina's attention and she nodded again. — 'I have HIV. I don't use the phrase "I am HIV positive" as my identity is not wrapped up in this one thing. I have a law degree, I have HIV, I have a good job, I enjoy art, I xyz — all parts of my identity. Sometimes important, sometimes background noise.'

'I know,' said Tina and then added, 'I'm sorry to interrupt.'

'No, it's okay,' said Austin.

'It's just that I don't want people saying all the time my daughter is HIV positive. We don't need it to be pointed out. It's not even her fault.' Tina almost immediately realised the callousness of this. Her mouth turned downwards. 'I'm sorry, I didn't mean any offence.'

Nick spoke up now. 'It's okay. None of us are to blame. It's not anyone's fault if they get it. Because anyone *can* get it.' He twisted in his chair. 'I know this because my Jamal taught it to me. I came into my relationship thinking this guy would never accept me if he knew, but once I told him he was okay with it. He just wanted me to stay healthy.'

'Except that it's not the whole story,' Waldron sighed, 'because saying HIV, at least in certain circles, is like saying "sinner", "victim card", "hooker", "fag", "slut" and a few other choice phrases. And that, coupled with the fact you have all suffered, because of and despite of having the virus, means it's hard to talk about it sometimes.'

'Absolutely!' Austin said. 'Romantic relationships are another minefield. When to disclose, if to disclose, how to disclose, on and on. I mean I'm not dating ... now ... and this freaks me out.'

Nick smiled. 'This sounds trite, but it gets better, bro, it really does.'

Austin wanted to believe this to be true. He was surprised how calm he'd been thus far. Only ten minutes ago, he might have given anything to not open up to these people. His mother, Zara, his clients, these were all the drama queens he'd known in his life and they had all been more than enough. He was puzzled to be the one feeling the need to let it all out. So, he did.

'... So that's it: I have HIV, I'm getting treatment, and it's one part of my identity. I'm trying not to let it weigh on me.'

Everyone clapped. And where he normally found his clapping banal, almost childish, Austin now felt glad for it, happy to be surrounded by people who understood.

That afternoon, Austin met Nick and Jamal at a pub opposite Kings Cross station. This bar was so different from the ones in East London where Noah liked to roam, that as Austin sat on the plush velvet chairs sipping a vodka-based cocktail, he couldn't help thinking he had fallen into a better group of people.

Jamal pushed his glasses up on his handsome nose and smiled. It was the first time Austin ever saw him smile with the fullness of his mouth, and he at once became less tense. So, Jamal wouldn't hold things against him.

'I wondered how you were coping, Austin?' Jamal asked. 'I did ask Nick about you, but he doesn't like to talk about the group much. He always goes on about —'

'— Patient confidentiality,' Nick said finishing his partner's sentence.

This made Austin chuckle, considering how much of his own client's confidentiality he violated on a daily basis in regular gossip text sessions with Nick.

He considered the question for a moment as he sank into his chair. 'Actually, I think I'm starting to do okay.'

'Who gave it to you anyway?'

'Jamal! Oh my god.'

'Shit, is that too much?'

'Yes, I mean, no, it's okay.' Austin gulped down the remainder of his cocktail. 'I was dating this Bangladeshi guy called Noah ...'

'South Asian. Nice,' said Jamal and put his hands out to illustrate the relative size of a man's cock.

Austin, who wasn't used to such behaviour, frowned a little, but then carried on talking.

'Well, anyway, he wasn't ever faithful. I don't know exactly how many people he slept with, but he gave it to me.'

'Why do you say "people"? Is he into girls too?' asked Jamal, and then without waiting for answer said, 'Playa, playa!' and again made the same gesture with his hands only this time the size grew longer.

Nick slapped Jamal on the chest. 'Have a little sympathy, eh, Jay?'

'I think you'll find the better phrase is "empathy,"' said Jamal, 'and I'm just trying to make light of it. Dealing with your disease is not easy.'

Austin felt a pang of envy. Their relationship banter was lovely to witness. He worried if he would ever find that kind of playfulness with someone.

'How did you react when you found out Nick had it?' He leaned in closely to Jamal, almost mouthing the question.

'Well the thing is,' — Jamal picked up his drink and took a sip. — 'I was really, really awful to guys before about this kind of thing.'

'How so?'

'For instance, I once hooked up with this guy at a party —'

Nick wiggled in his chair and made a sour face. Austin wasn't sure if this was because he didn't want to hear about Jamal's past or if it was because he'd already heard it too many times before.

'— and then a couple days later he told me he was poz, so I wrote him back something like "Sorry, I'm clean and want to stay that way" ... I mean I didn't think about what I was saying, it was only gut instinct.'

Austin let out a pregnant sigh. This was the reaction he feared most.

'But do you know how utterly ignorant that was of me?' Jamal motioned toward Nick. 'When I met this guy, he changed my life and I realised that words like "clean" suggest that a poz person is unclean, therefore dirty. It's the idea you can't touch them or show any kind of intimacy, otherwise you'll also almost definitely get infected with the virus —'

'And you'll all turn into zombies!' Nick said, putting his arm around his partner.

'— and honestly, your chances of being exposed to HIV are significantly lower when hooking up with a poz guy who has an undetectable viral load than someone who may not know or be honest about his status.'

'That much is clear,' said Austin, shaking his head.

'If you want my advice ...,' Jamal said now.

But Austin wasn't sure he did. He remembered his mother using that very phrase when he and Noah broke-up; that only ended with a bad hang-over.

'... You have to make things right with Noah. You won't ever feel settled in yourself until you do.'

'Jay's right,' said Nick. 'One of the best things I ever did was to confront Harry.'

'Wait, what?! *The* Harry, as in the one I met at your birthday?'

'Yea, that's him.' Jamal exhaled.

'But he never even knew he had it, you see,' said Nick then to ease things over. 'So, by telling him I not only helped myself feel better but I pretty much saved Harry's life. Maybe it would've been too late for him otherwise.'

'Absolutely fucking incredible,' said Austin. 'But you see, I already tried to speak to him once. I confronted him and he denied everything.'

'But it's not about confrontation.' Nick looked with earnest at Austin.

'He's right,' said Jamal. 'You think because he lied to you that he's worthless now? Or worse yet, you think *you're* worthless? That's just wrong, mate, flat out.'

Austin moved his tongue to the roof of his mouth in protest, but no words formed.

'Love is not some elixir that plasters over bad intentions or petty secrets. Maybe he never told you because he is scared. Or maybe he's an arse-hole. I don't know. All I know is if you don't say something, don't try to make it right, you'll never feel whole in yourself. The most important things are buried in your mind; you just have to use the treasure map of your heart to find them.'

Late the next day, Austin made his way to East London. He had never been to Noah's flat, and it occurred to him how strange this was. It would have been perfectly normal to want to see where your boyfriend lived, to want to spend time there, maybe stay the night occasionally. He wondered why he never made a big deal of this when they were together. Shouldn't that have set off some alarm bells or warning signals? How naive I am, he thought, how utterly blind. And yet he kept walking toward the street where Noah lived. Jamal was right: a little bit outside of his mind was where Austin had been living since his diagnosis, and what is the mind without the heart?

Once at the correct building, Austin rang the intercom labelled Hakim. He fiddled with his clothing and peered into the reflection of the glass door while the bell resonated. After an inordinately long time, a voice came over the intercom, but not one Austin recognised.

'Umm hello, I'm looking for Noah Hakim. Does he live here?'

'Who's asking?' the husky voice replied.

'It's an old ...' — he wondered what he should call himself — 'old friend of his: Austin.'

'Don't talk nonsense,' the voice blustered.

'Sorry?'

'Is that really you, Austin?'

'Noah?!'

A buzzer unlatched the door and a few moments later Austin found himself face-to-face with Noah for the first time in months. He had changed in those days since the break-up, before Austin's diagnosis. Now he appeared as a muscular, balding man rather than the brooding boy with hard features with never much to say. His voice sounded richer, as though he'd gone through some sort of second puberty. Austin was at once compelled to kiss this strange, exotic creature but at the same time could recognise something of the old Noah in

those arrogant eyes twinkling a little too knowing-
ly as they exchanged cool greetings.

'But why?' asked Noah. 'Why are you here?
How did you know to find me here?'

'Last year I asked you for your address so I
could send a birthday card. I saved it in my
phone.'

Noah's eyes raised. 'Ever the organised one.'

I never even got a thank you, Austin remembered now. But he understood this to be what acceptance meant: coming to terms with those that
have hurt you and acknowledging the ways you've
hurt yourself.

'And why are you here?' Noah asked again, this
time with more force.

Austin looked around the apartment. On the
mantelpiece sat a photo of their trip to Florence.
There were free weights scattered around the
sofa. A small vase with decorative flowers painted
on it sat atop the coffee table. Next to it a worn-
looking debit card was laid next to a piece of
notebook paper folded into a siphon.

'So I can be free,' he said.

'Look, I don't know what you're on about,
babe, and I don't want to know.' Noah's face became red and the veins on his forehead stuck out.

'You just called me babe.' Austin's voice
cracked.

'No, I didn't, Austin. Don't mess with me.'

'No, you did. I mean, yes, you did and I'm not messing with you.'

'Well slip of the tongue,' said Noah with full knowledge of the fact he'd said it. He marvelled at how he regressed back into old habits of speaking to Austin. This scared him, and he looked down at the ground, back up at Austin, and down at the ground once more.

Austin surveyed the flat again. There was no sign of Noah's sister. He wondered if she'd already gone off to uni.

'What I have realised,' said Austin, looking at the top of Noah's receding hairline, 'is I've got to make things right with you if I'm ever going to be able to move on with my life.' He paused waiting for a response, but when one wasn't forthcoming, he continued: 'And all I want is to just be able to live. Not to think about this every day. Just to live.'

After some time, Noah looked up. At once the springtime of life returned to his face. His hair was still balding and he was rather more fit than Austin remembered him, but something about his face now changed. Had, in fact, become more familiar to Austin. His voice too softened when he spoke. 'I forgive you, Austin.'

With a rage that could only have been inherited from his mother, Austin flew across the room at Noah. Grabbing him by his firm right bicep, Austin shouted, 'And what the hell does that mean?!'

'Let me go!'

Unrelenting, Austin barked: 'I don't need your forgiveness, mate. Not *your* bloody forgiveness.' His enunciation grew elongated as though he sat in judgement of Noah. And then swiftly, he added: 'I want retribution.'

As Austin shouted, Noah reached his left hand behind his back and pushed away Austin's hold on his arm.

'What? You thought you could hold me down, son?' Noah said this in an almost childish half-whisper.

Noah's words made Austin jump. By instinct he bolted from the flat. Minutes later, he stood outside on the pavement again. His armpits were sweaty, fear excreting from his pours. Using his shirt to wipe the sweat from his forehead, he began to cross the road in the direction of the tube station. He put his hand into the inside pocket of his jacket to pull out his mobile phone. Without looking up, he began to dial his mother's number. As he was about to punch the green call button, a car swung around the corner. It couldn't have been travelling more than twenty miles per hour and yet the impact on Austin's lower half was immediate. His legs buckled beneath his body, coming to rest near his waist. He lay still on the pavement, his body unmoving save for his eyes which filled with tears. A small pool of blood seeped from his limbs and surrounded both kneecaps. As Austin's eyelids began to close, he contemplated how unfair it all seemed. Even in that moment, he knew it was irrational, blaming himself now, when he'd just been hit by a car, for what happened. But he couldn't shake the feeling that this was it. Karma come to take him for not making amends, for becoming the bad guy instead of the peacemaker he sat out that afternoon to be. As he lost consciousness, his last thoughts were of forgiveness.

The metal arm rails of the emergency room bed dug into Austin's forearms. The smell of two-parts antiseptic, one-part body odour were familiar to him, and waking now he could recognise almost instinctively he was in Chelsea and Westminster Hospital. The place had a certain mystique about it. The nurses traded encouraging smiles with the patients. The patients blew their noses, held their bellies, spat into spittoons on a regimented cycle. Family members and friends sat in the lobby tapping their feet impatiently and rhythmically to the slow jazz playing over the PA system. Everyone initiated small talk to make the time go by faster, even those usually loathe to speak to strangers.

Austin rubbed his eyes, flicking specks of sleep from the corners. 'What are you in for?' he said to the patient in the gurney to the right of his own. He thought of hospitals, especially this one with its HIV treatment clinic, as prisons, everyone biding their time until parole.

'Cancer,' said Patient R, a woman in her late forties who looked worryingly thin, her bronze skin pulled tight over her bones. 'I take cancer meds and I sometimes have bad side-effects. Nausea, mostly. This time it was pretty bad, I can't seem to keep solid foods down.' There were tubes protruding from the veins on her arms.

'Pfff, that's nuffin',' said the patient to the left of Austin now, an elderly white man, as if anyone asked his opinion. 'Heart disease runs in my family. I swore I was having a heart attack, but the doc stuck me in here, and I'm still kicking, so I guess everything is A-Okay, can't never be too careful at my age, heart attacks everywhere you look, every fortnight I think I'm going to have one, but here I am still kicking, junior doctors pulling me through, God bless this great country.'

Like Jesus with two fellow convicts on each side, one good-hearted and the other not, Austin weighed up his options.

'I've got HIV,' he said now to Patient R. It was the first time he ever uttered those words to any stranger outside of the support group. It was liberating. 'I'm on ART. Anti-retrovirals. When I first got the script, the pharmacist said it's likely if you're sick the first time you have a drug, it will probably make you sick each time you have it.'

Despondency clouded Patient R's features. 'Frankly, honey,' she said, 'taking meds sucks.'

Patient L chewed on his bottom lip. His skin looked splotchy, and he needed a shave. 'Orderly! Orderly!' he screamed. 'We got two whiners in here!'

The man's theatrics started to wear on Austin. He stared down at his hands, twisting and knotting them. Doing so held back the turmoil inside. Despair roamed the room, expelled on the breath of worriers like him as well as those doing their best to bite down on the pain that brought them there.

'But you look beat up, honey. Did something else happen?'

Recognition came to his face. 'The car,' he said aloud.

'Car?' asked Patient R.

'I think — no, I know — it hit me ...' He put his hands on his stomach and yelped out in pain. His once-defined abs now moved like a slab of butter, firm on the edges but squishy in the middle. '... I just can't recall anything else.'

'Thank God you're alive, honey.'

Indeed, thought Austin. He wondered where Noah had been when the accident happened.

He had a choice. The goal: quick and painless. Blowing his head off was too messy and besides, he didn't have a gun. Slitting his wrist seemed easy, but fraught with unnecessary agony. He could jump off a building — maybe one of those skyscrapers in Canary Wharf with viewing balconies — but he was scared he might regret the decision half-way down, and who wants to spend the last few seconds of their life in regret? An overdose of prescription painkillers would do the trick, but where would he get them without any money and what if they didn't work? He'd heard about people's stomachs being pumped.

So, it was settled. He would hang himself. Rope was easy to come by and he could leave his body there dangling, waiting for someone to find him. It seemed much more courteous than any other option where his blood might be spilt. Noah had always been this way, at least in his own estimation of himself: courteous to a fault.

He read the self-help articles. Hell, he even called the suicide hotline. None of it helped. Not that help was what he was looking for. No, what he wanted was a way out.

It was that Sunday afternoon when he decided to go through with it. Two Saturdays prior, everything had been fine. But not fine, tolerable. And then the blackout happened. He quit going to work that Monday and stopped answering calls and texts on Tuesday. By the time Austin paid his visit, Noah was too far gone.

After a call to the suicide helpline, speaking to someone called Tom, Noah began talking to himself. He would murmur words of reassurance, almost in a whisper. Everything is fine, he'd say aloud. You are stronger than what you are feeling. At about the same time, he began reading from the Quran, methodically working his way from sura to sura. Defiling the sacred book, he underlined Äyah 64.9: *The day when He will gather you ... that is the day of mutual blaming.*

He found himself reciting the verse over and over, pacing from corner to corner of his studio. Reciting the Quran, taking a line from the coffee table, walking aimlessly to the other end of the flat, and doing it all over again. A circuit of scripture-drugs-scripture repeated in sets of ten, twenty, sometimes thirty rounds. All this went on for the better part of a week. In between circuits, he ate ramen noodles, drank whatever liquor he could find in the refrigerator and cupboards, and binge-watched South Park episodes. Anything to stop thinking about what he'd done to Austin.

On Sunday he ran out of visible options. All the ramen packets were gone. He drank the last beer, he thought, last night after reciting the sura; but he couldn't quite keep track of time. He watched every South Park series, some of them more than once. He fast-forwarded through most of the early We killed Kenny episodes. Now, waking up on Sunday maybe mid-morning, maybe early afternoon — he couldn't tell which and long stopped charging his mobile phone, the only clock in the flat — he knew he must do it. I wish people knew just how bad things were in my head when I think about jumping from some skyscraper somewhere or when I just want to ram pills down my throat, he murmured waking from a terrifying dream of Austin dying inch-by-inch from some AIDS-defining illness. A lot of people call suicide a coward's way out — this was another voice in his head, a deeper one with more colour, a voice he didn't recognise — but they don't realise how bad you are until they have lost someone close. Yea! You've got to show them — a third voice called out, this one was feminine and full of rage. The kind of rage he always associated with the caricature of an angry black woman. But he didn't think to question to whom these other voices belonged or what they wanted of him. It all felt natural, orderly and natural. Like the Comanche worrier he pictured before, he must protect himself and to protect the people he loved, especially Austin. Offences required punishment, and no satisfaction could be given to avert this need. He would give his own life to save Austin's.

He flung the thick, fibrous rope around the light fixture in the living room. Go on then, make a noose! — the deep voice rang inside his mind. He poked the end of the rope through the top of a loop. Now climb into it, don't be a punk bitch! — this was the angry female voice now. As though in a shock-induced trance, he obeyed the voices, climbing onto a chair and pulling his head into the rope. The noose was like the dirt of the earth, his head like a dandelion poking up through the roots. The voices went away, and the call of the void echoed through him. He kicked the chair and fell with a violent twist. His neck jerked to one side and held his cold body tightly in mid-air. He lurched as though a seizure erupted from his brain and spread all the way down to his toes. Before his eyes drooped to a close, he fixated on a picture frame atop the mantel. It was the photo of him and Austin in Florence. As the oxygen to his brain cut off, he thought: What have I done?

Doctor Tandy Newman, a frail and friendless old man, was awakened by the ache in his right leg. His knee long-ago gave way to a replacement alloy of cobalt-chromium and titanium, leaving him with a dull pain in the calf almost every morning. 'What an existence,' he grumbled aloud to no one. Sometimes he could still picture Mrs Newman, dead eighteen months now, lying in the bed next to him. Newman should have taken his pension last year, when he was legally allowed to do so, but thought what the hell, he'd give it another go, and besides helping to mend other people somehow made him feel less miserable about this own ailing body and solitary existence.

Still two hours before dawn, Newman pulled his old Ford Escort into the private parking lot of the Chelsea and Westminster Hospital. His first visit, before his rounds or his English Breakfast, was always the first-floor chapel. Kneeling at the altar surrounded by stained glass windows, Newman looked up at the painting by Giotto which he admired day-after-day in his twenty-five years working there. He lowered his head, leaned forward, and put his elbows on the pedestal as though to get this thing ironed out between him and God.

'I'm lousy today,' he prayed. 'I'm just way off, in every way.'

He looked up again at the painting. Fresh like his first time seeing it. The foreground of the canvas was covered in gold leaf, a clear link to the panel's origin as a precious religious icon. Closing his eyes, he began to picture himself as a subject in the painting, one of the minor saints perhaps surrounding the virgin and child. He imagined himself looking on at Mary, seeing her face in the flesh, as it were, and wishing he could join her at the right hand of Christ. His eyelids unfastened again.

'Holy Mary, Mother of God . . . I entrust all my care and pain to you.'

For a fraction of a second, the candles on the altar flickered and Mary's face sparkled. Dr Newman thought that today he'd be okay; today he'd make it through another round.

Kneeling had become easier since the knee replacement but getting up became harder with age. As he pulled himself up from the altar, he wondered who his first patient would be.

Austin had been transferred to an in-patient room the previous night. He awoke that morning wondering who Patient R was and what became of her in the hours since he was moved upstairs as she was left waiting on an attending doctor in the Accident and Emergency department. She needed the help more than I do, he thought.

Down the hall, Tandy Newman hung his winter coat in exchange for a long white one. He looked at the patient rota handed to him by a nurse. She was a pretty blonde girl, and Newman couldn't help thinking she looked like his Marjorie did when they first met.

'First case is a tough one,' said the nurse, with a continual demeanour of circumspection about her. 'HIV patient hit by a car yesterday morning. He's transferred in from A&E.'

'How did he get to hospital?'

The nurse picked up the patient's chart. 'Says somebody called an ambulance; doesn't state who.'

'Is the chap badly hurt?'

'More emotionally than physically, I'd say. He crushed a rib, but the attending physician sta-bilised it.'

These few odd facts, in the telling of them, sounded simple enough, but in Newman's mind they didn't register as discrete truths at all. At sixty-six, he was old enough to have lived and worked through the worst of the AIDS epidemic, losing no less than three friends in the process, two of them ostensibly — and against all media hype — straight, white men with wives and children. HIV played no favourites. Tandy Newman was also no stranger to emotional damage in his patients. 'It's all in your head' became a favourite phrase over his decades of working in healthcare. The reality, he surmised, was that all pain whether caused by a broken rib, a bad heart, or a poor lifestyle is processed in the brain, right alongside the part regulating emotion. And therefore, unlike most of his younger, more hard-boiled colleagues, Newman practised a more traditional way of medicine: always making it a point to try to address a patient's mental as well as physical pain.

From the frame of the door, the patient sat idly in room 305 looked well enough. His toes were sticking out from beneath the wool-blend blanket and he seemed to be either meditating or daydreaming, his glare intense and straight-forward. But to Newman's way of thinking, first impressions do not, contrary to popular belief, form lasting impressions. And on looking closer, what he saw didn't seem so good. The patient's light brown hair was damp and sporadically matted to his head. And as Newman moved closer to examine the patient, who was wet with sweat, he noticed small water droplets falling from both the patient's eyes.

'Don't be alarmed. I'm the consultant sent to treat you.' Austin gave a lopsided grin as he shifted his thoughts from Patient R to the doctor now stood before him.

'Oh, uhmm, sorry, doctor, it's not you; I am just thinking about something; someone else.'

'And who might that be,' — he looked at the patient's chart — 'Austin?'

He looked away, light-headed. 'That's a little bit personal, no?'

'I wondered if I could help at all?'

Austin drew in a long breath. 'I wish you could.'

Newman could see the nurse was right. 'Try me.'

'Well ... there was another patient; she was with me in A&E. I just wondered what happened to her. But I don't know her name, so it doesn't matter.'

Newman rubbed his forehead. Austin toyed with the idea of telling the doctor more but stopped short.

'I am sure I could find out if she's alright,' he said and scribbled something in the chart. Austin sat motionless. 'So, tell me about your injury. What happened?'

'I can't remember much, to be honest. I was leaving a, uhm, a friend's place and I vaguely remember a car coming at me, but then the next thing I recall is waking up here, with the lady I told you about on one side of me and some chav on the other.'

Newman chuckled. 'We do get our fair share of chav around here, I'm afraid. I sometimes feel I'm in an episode of The Only Way is Essex.'

'You know that series?' Austin let loose a slow smile that built as the surprise sank in. 'Sorry! I didn't think guys your age watch that sort of thing!' Newman bounced on the heel of his hospital-grade orthopaedic shoes. 'Sorry again,' said Austin blushing.

'Well medicine is a jealous mistress,' said Newman. 'I need something to help unwind now, don't I?'

Austin's face was outright beaming now, and despite the predicament of his present situation he felt better than he had in weeks.

'Anyway,' he said some moments later, 'I don't remember anything else. The doc yesterday said I've got a broken rib; that's about all I know.'

He can laugh though, thought the doctor. A broken rib would hurt like hell if you tried laughing. Tandy Newman knew the diagnoses made by Accident and Emergency were often incomplete, and sometimes just plain wrong. There was only so much that could be figured out in an emergency room despite the best efforts of his junior colleagues.

'We'll do a few more tests to figure out the damage done, Austin. And don't worry about not remembering. This is absolutely normal.'

Austin stiffened, and Newman made to explain further.

'It's called anterograde amnesia. The loss of ability to form memories for a period of time after an accident. Think of it as a coping mechanism.'

'That sounds serious!'

'As a matter of fact, no,' said Newman adopting a subtler tone. 'You are HIV positive, aren't you?' he asked, obviously knowing the answer.

Austin reddened. 'I *have* HIV,' he said, 'I don't own it.'

'In any case, what happened after the accident is not altogether different, I would guess, to what happened shortly after you first tested positive.'

Austin's brain rewound to that moment three months prior when he sat in the clinic in Westferry Road. The minutes and hours afterwards were a blur.

'How are you feeling today?' Newman asked.

'Overall okay. My body aches a bit, but if I hadn't been told otherwise, I don't think I'd even guess I'd been hit by a car.'

'Good, that's just fine then.' He consulted the chart once more. 'How about the Atripla? How's your tolerance been? Do you manage to take the drug on schedule?'

'The side effects — the dreams and hallucinations — like getting my arse handed to me on a tarnished silver platter, if you'll excuse the pun.'

The doctor nodded.

'But how do you know so much about HIV?' Austin wondered.

'I've been around a long-time.' Newman knew he was Austin's best shot today. Not for physical recovery — he was doing fine with that — but for emotional stability. There was also something in this young man that reminded Newman of himself. His work ethic had been one not based on science alone, but on faith. Faith in the human spirit, faith in the corporal body and its generative powers to heal itself. Still, he understood that to rely on faith was contemptible, when patients would suffer without some scientific intervention. Austin represented for him not just another patient, but a chance to impact on someone's life. He couldn't help but thinking that doing so might in some way impact on his own well-being.

'In fact,' he said with a sadness in his eyes, 'I think the world has seen too much disease and death as a result of this damned virus. I, uhm, we need you to survive. Not just to survive, but to thrive.'

Tandy Newman thought he said too much, but Austin's face began to glow.

'I think I'm tired of blaming myself.' Austin's mind raced with all the things he had tried in the last ninety days — eating well, getting enough rest, taking his medication on time, exercising. Each helped, in its own way, but none addressed the root cause. Once all the anger at Noah faded, what was left? Only guilt.

'Oh, my dear, never blame yourself.' He put his hand on Austin's back. 'Disease is indiscriminate.'

'You asked about the medicine? I take it every day.' Austin bit his lower lip and then smiled. 'If only there were a drug to take away the hurt.'

Newman pined for a golden age when bedside manner mattered more than the latest drug revolution. But he felt Austin's pain. The prospect of living with something that might kill you can incite more fear than actually being killed by it. But at the same time, knowing you have come close to death or are living with something that can kill paradoxically eases the fear of dying from it.

Grabbing Austin's hand with a surprising amount of force for a frail man, Dr Newman looked him in the eye. 'Listen to me. You must face your daemon every day; and defeat it. Fight the virus with prescribed medication, but moreover, fight it with your ability to remain bigger than it. It may pervade every blood cell in your body, but you cannot let it pervade your mind.'

Austin sat for a moment, examining the doctor, but came up with nothing to say.

As Newman turned to leave room 305, he delivered one final line to his first patient of the day: 'Oh, and I'll be sure to check on that lady you mentioned.'

Dr Tandy Newman did more for Austin in those twenty minutes than weeks of group counselling. Not that the therapists were to blame. Something changed. It could have been the doctor's kindly manner, his quick wit, his bedside manner. It didn't matter much to Austin. His mind permeated now with familiar senses: the smell of honeysuckle in his grandmother's garden, the taste of fine wine in Tuscany, his first kiss on a cool Spring day. He was moved by these sensations rushing into his corporal being, memories thrust in place by the doctor who took an interest, who dared, despite the rigidity of his profession, to share empathy — in fact, brotherhood — with a patient half his age. Austin believed he had not lost all of the poetry in his soul. He could still feel alive, could still awe at the majesty of living, apart from any sourness the disease and its origins brought about. He felt an ache — not the kind related to a fractured rib or to his broken heart. His soul ached. He wished he could give himself over to these past-present catechisms erupting in his mind. Just then, and not at all to his surprise (for her timing was always right), Zara entered the room. He jumped from the bed, giving her a tight hug.

Zara first saw the article announcing Noah's suicide in one of those daily newspapers thrown haphazardly on the seat of the Jubilee line train heading eastbound. It took her a moment to realise the young man referenced in the article, whose body had been discovered some twelve hours after he hung himself — this 'Mr Hakim, aged 29' — was in fact Austin's ex.

The article was accompanied by an undated photo of the suicide victim. He was forcing a smile and appeared to be standing near a large statue in front of an ornate building. Far to the right of the photograph, she noticed a foreshortened arm attached to a hidden hand wrapped around Noah's back. The photo had been cropped above the elbow, so although she couldn't see more than that little bit of flesh, she knew it was Austin in the missing half of the picture.

Zara spent the last quarter hour rehearsing what she might say to her best friend, how she might give the news to him delicately. Googling 'breaking bad news' on her Android was as far as she got before lashing out in a cold sweat. With Austin hugging her now, she relished the warmth of his body and wondered where his good spirits came from.

'Sit down,' she said calmly.

'Don't be silly, Z., I'm more than fine.'

She drew the newspaper out of her rucksack and handed it to him. He stood by the edge of bed, his shoulders curled over his chest. His heartbeat, which only moments ago beat with exhilaration, was now sluggish and grey.

Staring at the photo now, she said, 'It's like looking at a dream, isn't it?'

Austin's mind flittered between images. Noah hanging from a noose. Their silenced-filled first day in Florence. Dr Newman's firm grip. The juxtaposition made him dizzy and he collapsed into an armchair, folding the newspaper over his lap. 'It's a nightmare,' he said.

For the second time that day, Austin found nothing more to say. Some moments passed as he sat looking off into the distance.

'Did he do this to get back at me?' he asked finally, his cheeks turning red.

'No, I don't think so, love,' Zara replied, tears in her eyes. 'Maybe he just felt guilty. The article said there was drug paraphernalia and beer bottles lying around his flat. I think there was really something not right in his head.'

Austin frowned. At some point he must start taking responsibility for his own actions and for the role he played in the cards life dealt him, Zara thought. He had been on the right path — going to Noah's place had been a sound step on the road to recovery — but now she wondered if Austin would ever learn to look past his own protective bubble. She could predict his reaction. The accident would only reinforce his belief that the world was conspiring against him. She wanted to shake him, to force him into understanding how everything that happened to him in the last few months was connected, but she thought gentleness and empathy were what he needed most now.

'I know, I know,' she pulled him closer. 'What Noah did to you is unforgivable. If that were me, I mean, I don't believe I could forgive him, not even now.' She could see the hurt in Austin's eyes. 'But I also think it's okay if you want to grieve for him.'

'If guilt is what he felt, he shouldn't have.' Austin's knees shook. 'I forgive him, and I have to learn to forgive myself.' The shudder of his body moved as a mild electrocution; Austin sensed a sudden, strangeness that somewhere, someplace, maybe in another time, he would meet Noah again.

A dozen needles danced their way across Zara's forehead. Was she hearing him correctly? You can't just snap your fingers and say goodbye to well-established patterns, even when those patterns result in bad consequences.

Zara sat for a moment not quite sure what to make of it all. She expected Austin to burst into tears, to at least get angry, show some kind of emotion at Noah's passing. The sudden acceptance and forgiveness(!) on his part baffled her. Not so much for the fact it happened — of that she felt glad — but for the awareness that everything she thought she knew about Austin — she was, as far as she was concerned, his only real friend — had suddenly been called into question.

And then the two of them began to perform a speechless ritual that solidified Zara's belief she knew nothing, absolutely nothing, about anything to do with Austin. The latter didn't do speechless, and yet here he was silently passing her back the newspaper, she taking it and tucking into her handbag and then pouring him a cup of water from the hospital-issued pitcher. Austin grabbed the cup, drank and wondered why hospital water pitchers, the ugly shade of pinkish grey they are, held such comfort in their constant state of coolness. He imagined stealing one and later bragging about it to would-be, currently non-existent friends. Confession: I loved the water pitcher in my hospital room so much that I brought it home. I didn't think much of it, to be honest. Thought 'they don't reuse these, no?' His make-believe friends horrified. And why think of this now, he thought, but got no reply, so he stopped to examine the top of the newspaper sticking out of Zara's half-open purse.

'I just don't understand how he could get to this place.'

This was familiar territory now, something Zara could work with. 'From the standpoint of someone like you or me who is not suicidal, it is difficult to understand. But look at it from another perspective. Flip it around. Do you understand why your clients do the things they are accused of doing?'

Austin's eyebrows raised. 'I try to give them the benefit of the doubt. It's the best way I can defend them.'

'And I'm not asking you to defend Noah in any way. You can't really. But I think for someone to go against every single survival instinct in his body and act on those truly horrendous, awful, dark thoughts, whilst knowing the consequences of what he's about to do to himself, shows it's an illness and that it certainly is not a cry for attention.'

A single teardrop rolled down Austin's cheek. 'I loved him.'

Millicent Smith spent the entire morning combing through her tatty black address book. She once tried to add all the entries, line-by-line, into her phone contacts, but the chore was daunting and now with time against her, she needed to rely on old comforts.

Austin was in trouble. She could feel it in her bones as surely as she could still feel the presence of her long-gone husband roaming the halls, rattling her mind. A mother knows when her son is in danger.

She flipped to the Js. Jackson, Jacobson, Jeffries. Jeffries — now there was surname she hoped to forget.

There were a clan of Jeffries in Ohio. Ye shall know them by their fruits, and indeed you could also know them by their plain dress and chaste speech. Their women wore long garbs covering their temple garments and their men had bumper stickers on their cars which read *I'm a Mormon. I know it. I live it. I love it.* They were not subtle. But they were a kindly family. They'd never been in legal trouble, rarely caused much of a stir with the locals, and their children stayed out of the public schools. Their symbols of power were more innocuous — pamphlets handed out in front of the drug store on Main Street, missionary lesson manuals left not so discretely on the reception tables of local restaurants — all of which helped reassure them they were on their way to the celestial kingdom. As family patriarch Rufus Jeffries put it: 'As man now is, God once was. As God now is, man may be.'

Rufus took seriously his responsibility to create more potential gods. In this line of thought, children are more valuable than gold and none was more precious than child number one. In his case, a girl, Millicent Anne Jeffries.

By virtue of being female, Milli (as she came to be known) was the rare exception to the four C rules of the Mormon family: chastity, conjugality, children, and chauvinism. Whereas Mrs Jeffries was expected to stay home, cleaning, cooking, and raising the children (a further five were to come), Rufus took a more egalitarian approach to his first-born. Milli had been primed from an early age to join the church's missionary movement. It was made very clear that her mission was to be one of proselytising and given her ingratiation with church doctrine, the young Millicent soon took this to mean 'white is good, other colours are bad and need saving.'

Millicent's whiteness was grounded in a retro vision of the midwestern state of the United States she grew up in, one of white picket fences and stay-at-home mothers, fathers unashamed of working hard for corporate America, offspring who were silent unless spoken to. How do you have such perfect, beautiful, well-behaved, high-performing children? A question she heard asked to her parents on more than a few occasions. Don't you just envy us? Her mother would respond.

But as she got older, Milli began to ask questions. A keen reader, she took an interest, within the limited selection of books in the village library, in personal narratives, her favourite being Thoreau. One day at Sacrament meeting when the focus was on Jesus and his atoning sacrifice, Milli felt the spirit of the Lord. Imagining a transcendental experience like in *Walden*, she mentioned this to her bishop, who rebuked her. 'You are commanded to search the scriptures, not the library,' he said. In disillusionment, she left temple that day in search of another way.

Baptists, Pentecostals, Catholics. They all tried to convert her. But they were all fundamentalists. This simple fact did more to turn Milli away from religion than any Billy Graham crusade, See You at the Pole rally, or Friday night revival could ever have hoped to accomplish. It was no surprise, then, when she met Thomas, a sprightly young English atheist, at a petrol station the summer of her eighteenth year, she pounced on his invitation for a beer on Saturday night. It didn't matter that (a) she wasn't allowed out after dark, or (b) she never took a drop of alcohol in her life. All that mattered was he offered a way out, if temporarily, from her miserable, fundamental existence. His accent hadn't hurt his chances either.

The Saturday beer outing came and went as well as Milli could have hoped. Sure, she'd thrown-up all over Thomas's Burberry coat, but he hadn't seemed to mind. Where Millicent was provincial, clumsy, almost amateurish, Thomas was worldly and dexterous. His hair fell down in titian locks, and when he pecked her on the cheek (for her breath still smelled of vomited beer) she blushed so intensely she thought she might explode like Violet Beauregarde. They were married three weeks later and on an airplane to Gatwick within four. She left her small town and all its fundamentalism behind and never looked back, except when it came to family values. The roots of Midwestern existence proved too deep to completely shake.

Changing her name to Smith — more upwardly mobile, less American, more English! — Milli set out to be the perfect wife. The problem was that everything Millicent knew about being a wife, she had learned from her mother.

Now a mother herself, Milli needed to save her son. Where was he? The Daily Mail report had scared her to the core. She recognised the grimy face in the photo on page four. It was that Islamist her son dated. But she wasn't without heart. Fundamentalist he may have been and certainly the world was better off without another one of *them*, but she was damned if she would let her own flesh and blood be torn away from her by this. Thomas leaving her eight months pregnant was bad enough, she'd not lose the rest of her family —

which when it came down to it was the two of them. That's what death is for, she thought, bringing people together.

Johnson. There it was. Marissa Johnson, an old friend from the Northwest London Ladies Bridge Club.

'It's Milli Jeffries, errr Smith,' she said into the phone receiver.

'Oh Milli, dear, how are you?' They hadn't spoken for the better part of a year.

'Fine, fine.' No time for small talk. 'Listen, you work for the NHS hospital in Chelsea, yes? ... Good, because I need some help. My son's gone missing and he's a regular patient of a clinic there ...' (She refrained from saying which one) '... I know, I know, patient privacy and so forth, but couldn't you make an exception for your old bridge partner, love? ... Oh dear! ... Room 305 did you say?'

And with that Millicent Smith née Jeffries threw on her coat and ran for the number 14 bus.

From Green Park to Chelsea and Westminster Hospital is a twenty-nine-minute journey. Milli arrived there in such a state that the reception desk could have been forgiven for mistaking her for a psychiatric patient rather than a concerned parent. What she hadn't counted on was a certain

Dr Tandy Newman being quicker to release Austin from hospital than she was to catch the double-decker. So, ten minutes later, she was on the number fourteen again, this time transferring at South Kensington for the District line and then for the Jubilee line, finally alighting at Swiss Cottage some forty-two minutes later, where she ran the five hundred metres from the station to Austin's flat and, finding no one home, sat herself on the stoop of the building. That rain drops were falling on her head and face was of no concern.

Walking up the pavement a quarter of an hour later, Zara was the first to spot Austin's mother soaking wet.

'If it isn't the famous Mrs Smith.' Zara hooked her hand under Austin's forearm, comforting and claiming him.

'It's okay, Z.,' Austin said, picking up his pace. 'It's nice to see you, mum.'

There was more wrapped up in those six words than Austin could ever have imagined. To Milli, who spent most of her existence trying to please men — her father, the church, her husband, her son — *It's nice to see you* really meant *I appreciate everything you've ever done for me and anything you might ever do in the future.* It was the gratification she deserved.

'Oh, my darling son!' She said this with such affectation that Austin at first wondered if some maleficent being had taken over his mother's voice box. She pushed Zara's hand away as she hugged Austin.

A few minutes later, the three of them sat in Austin's lounge sipping PG Tips. 'Don't you have anything from Fortnum's, dear?' She still sounded like a Stepford wife.

'I'm afraid not, mum.' He tried to keep from rolling his eyes. 'You never seemed to mind before.'

'How did you hear about Austin's accident anyway, Mrs Smith?' Zara asked then, sensing the need to break up a potentially awkward conversation.

'Well I'm his mother, aren't I?' Millicent's Midwest accent reappeared. It was now her turn to roll her eyes as she went on to explain how her day developed to finding herself there.

Turning her attention to her own copy of The Daily Mail, Milli read aloud: '*Man found dead in E. London, Apparent Suicide.*' Zara and Austin stared at her, willing her to stop but also somehow impressed she took such an interest. 'Well I just knew he was trouble.' When she got no reaction to this statement, she continued reading. '*Police say the man was found with drug paraphilia. No sui-*

cide note was present.' She looked up again, eager for a response.

Sensing this wouldn't end until she got one, Zara spoke up. 'I don't think we can put too much stock into The Daily Mail, though, surely.'

A look of condescension rolled across Milli. 'And why's that, dearie?'

'Jesus,' said Austin, actually rolling his eyes this time.

'I don't see what He has to do with it.'

'Well, look,' said Zara, careful not to get too preachy but obviously not her best friend's mother's biggest fan, 'they just can't be trusted. Take this as an example: a few years back, they ran a cover story along the lines of *London Underground infested with billions of human fleas.*'

'This has got to be good,' said Austin, a huge fan of both Zara's infinite pop culture wisdom and his mother being put in her place.

'Some news neutrality outfit contacted London Underground to ask them if the story was true and they said that no, of course it wasn't; so, the outfit asked where The Daily Mail would have gotten this figure of billions of human fleas ...'

'Are you going somewhere with this?' asked Millicent, with only a hint of disdain smeared across her dewy face.

'If you'd let me finish ...'

'Ah, I remember this now,' Austin chimed in. 'One of the big law firms handled the documentation. London Underground had put out a tender for interested bidders to manage the city's infestation control programme.'

'Exactly, and the tender mentioned there *would be* billions of human fleas on the tube *if* there were no infestation control programme in place.'

Milli's expression changed; she looked puzzled now. 'So, there are not billions of human fleas on the subway?' She still called it 'the subway' in true American fashion.

'Categorically, no.'

Austin's mother slid into a slump and then tried to cover it up by returning to a straighter posture. She had been defeated.

'Well let's check The Guardian, shall we?' said Austin, pulling out his iPhone. To his own wonderment, he wanted to make his mother feel better. Although it was taking a small miracle to keep himself from falling apart, it meant something that she was *trying*. After all she still stood dripping wet with rainwater and although it annoyed him she'd tracked mud from the stoop through the lobby, up the lift, from the flat door to the sofa on which she now sat, he nonetheless wanted to tend to her emotional fragility.

'Thank you, son, that sounds sensible.'

Austin looked toward his mother. He gave her a weak and caring smile and read: '*Police are investigating the death of a man after he was found in his home under suspicious circumstances ...* Why "suspicious circumstances"? He bloody killed himself.'

She sat for a moment, wriggling her fingers through one another. 'In my day,' she began as though she were ancient, 'suicide was seen as an ugly, loaded word. Maybe it still is. It's something of an ugly thing to do.'

Austin lowered his glance. He looked his mother squarely in her blue eyes, the same colour as his own. 'Death is harsh enough as it is. It's a good thing the newspaper avoided the term.'

Even Zara acquiesced now, dropping her formality. 'What else does the article say?'

Returning to the iPhone screen, Austin scanned the article and began to tremble. He placed his hand on his mother's thigh, inaugurated to serve as his balance. 'But I don't get it. The article says he is survived by a mother, father, and two brothers. He told me about a younger sister studying at Leicester.'

'Take it from someone with experience,' Millicent said. 'Some boys have a talent for bending the truth in ways too unbelievable to *not* be believed.'

She said this with such force that it moved Austin to put his head down on her shoulder. He felt like crying but having thought he'd done too much of that already, he simply soaked in the warmness of his mother's comfort.

Millicent Smith did not know what to do with such displays of affection. Although she often pursued it, it was foreign to her, this sense of being needed. Her real flair was not for fondness but for persistence. In times of other people's need, Milli's tenacity was quashed. Having obtained all she was after, there was nothing left to hope for. And so, she gently and politely removed her son's head from her shoulder and nodded to Zara. Giving an awkward wave goodbye, she slammed the door of flat 83 on her way out.

On each side of the casket sat two large candles. Both were white in colour. Above the coffin stood a bunch of white lilies interspersed with greenery. And in the background, faintly heard, a song in Arabic played over loudspeakers. Austin hated the song. It wasn't even a song, it was a man reciting the Quran in such a melodic tone that it made his ears cringe. They were not supposed to be here, at a funeral in this manner of Western tradition, but it was this or nothing, that was the deal Aashirbaad Hakim made with his wife. His son would not — could not — have a proper Muslim burial. He would get the funeral of his wife's people. The white man's funeral. That the Quran was recited at all had been a concession.

Austin sat in the back row of the funeral parlour with his head bowed. From the periphery of his eyes, a cross-hatch of maroon and pink dotted the carpet. It was nauseating. He looked up, letting his eyes roam over the wooden box up front. There should be a picture over the casket, he thought, of Jesus or the apostles. And then realising how ignorant this was, he felt ashamed and put his head down again. But what did he know of funeral homes? The whole setup was so bland, so uninviting that its physicality added to the collective grief.

As she walked to the front of the room and stood beside her son's closed casket, Lilly radiated with a glow that vibrated through Austin. So much so that one would hardly appreciate she was in mourning. She wore no burqa today; auburn curls cascading down her neck and shoulders framed her rigid but over-made-up face.

'My son was an evasive person,' she said. It was an odd beginning to a eulogy. 'I suppose this might be self-evident to those that knew him, but to his father and to myself, it came as a surprise.'

Two small tears formed in the ducts of either eye. She quickly wiped them away.

'I never thought I'd be doing this. A mother shouldn't have to, not in this way ...'

Austin put his head down again. The frog lodged in his chest jumped up and down. He gasped. The first tear fell down his cheek. The others followed in an unbroken stream.

'... When Noah was twelve, I found him one day in his room with a comic book. My husband dislikes all sort of representational art, so I wondered how Noah had gotten hold of the comic. Did a school friend give it to him? I asked. No, he said, he had saved up his weekly allowance of fifty pence. A half-pound isn't much, but it's all we could afford at the time, and I knew then my son would grow up to be resourceful. Nothing could stop him from getting what he wanted ...'

Aashirbaad groaned. Every synapse in his brain signalled at him to shout, to cry, to throw something. But he sat and groaned quietly, tightly wrapping his arms around each of his two living boys, one on either side. He hurt. He hurt more than he let on; more than his wife, he imagined.

'... I want to close by reading something somebody sent me yesterday.' Lilly pulled out a tiny bit of paper from the pocket of her long, black dress. Her throat thickened as she began to read.

Death is nothing at all. It does not count. I have only slipped away into the next room. Nothing has happened. Everything remains exactly as it was. I am I, and you are you, and the old life that we lived so fondly together is untouched, unchanged. Whatever we were to each other, that we are still.

Austin slipped out the door of the funeral parlour as soon as the service was over. It began to rain, and he did not, of course, have an umbrella. He whipped off his blazer and covered his head, running the third of a mile from the funeral parlour to the nearest tube station. If truth be told, he was happy for the rain. It merged with the tears which were still showering from his beet-red eyes.

A water main was broken at the corner of Forest Lane and Leytonstone Road. Giant puddles of water were exacerbated by the copious amount of rainfall. Austin was a soggy mess by the time he was pounding the discoloured brass knocker. Iman answered the door. At thirteen, he already wore a five-o'clock shadow and his hair was thinning. The resemblance to Noah washed over Austin like the fear of God descending on sinners.

'You're the man that came to Eid,' Iman said, giving Austin a look of recognition. 'Don't worry, mum's put the cat away for the day.'

The Hakim family house looked different in the daylight. The same six matching chairs were pushed against the walls of the dining room. But where the grand buffet had been set-up now a hodgepodge of all manner of food in mismatched containers was placed. Austin tensed. I should have brought something, he thought.

The house swarmed with warm bodies. Aasma Begum sat perched on one of the dining chairs in the corner of the room. Austin offered her a look of pity. A long drawl of a scowl crept onto her face. He turned to walk to the lounge across the corridor. Malabika and her husband were hovering on shaky stools in the dining room, the kind of stools more properly used for feet and not bottoms. Both of them were crouched over a tiny piece of paper, which from this distance Austin could make out as Noah's obituary. As he moved down the hallway near the back of the house, Austin noticed the kitchen door was open and so he peeked his head around the place where the wall abutted to the doorframe. Iman and the younger Hakim child were preoccupied with some sort of game. They sat silently passing back and forth a pair of playing cards, exchanging secretive glances. If you didn't know better, you wouldn't have guessed these boys had lost their older brother.

The kitchen faced south and as Austin stood there observing the Hakim children, the glare of a strong sun made a break in the rain, but it was only temporary. Soon the rain extended itself further and the sound of thunder could be heard in the distance.

'Is this real?' said Austin aloud, but got no response. He felt an odd déjà vu, a memory with no physical substance.

Lilly appeared from the hallway. Her burqa was on again and she looked more like herself, not only in dress but in mannerism. She stepped in front of him, blocking his way out of the diner.

'Astagfirullah, Austin, I didn't expect you here.'

Was she irritated? He couldn't be sure.

'I'm sorry, Mrs Hakim, for everything. I ... I ...' — he began to weep again — 'I just don't know what to say.'

Her back straightened. 'You think I'm some kind of fool?'

Austin moved a clenched fist across his eyeballs. 'I'm sorry?'

'Don't be,' she said, resuming her normal slouch, 'I know what was going on —'

Austin took a small step forward in the direction of the front door. He grew desperate.

Her voice became softer. '— between you and my son.' She almost whispered. 'Don't you worry about it. Mothers always know.'

Austin looked over Mrs Hakim's shoulder. Aashirbaad and Malabika were sat in the lounge discussing something. Aashirbaad's hands were moving wildly and he gave her a grievous smirk. Austin couldn't see Malabika's reaction through the yards of fabric wrapped round her face.

Lilly had been smiling, as much as her facial muscles would allow her today, but now she stopped. She could sense this was a conversation Austin did not want to have. She grabbed his hand and wrapped both of hers around it.

'I just want to say, I think you must have been good for him. You're the only friend he ever spoke about.'

He placed his other hand over hers. They stood face-to-face, hand-in-hand, an awkward dance of grieving souls.

'I hope so. I don't know anymore.'

'But I do,' she said.

Just then Aashirbaad got up from the lounge and walked past Austin and Lilly. He patted his wife on the shoulder but did not look Austin in the eye.

Austin's hands grew shaky. 'Your eulogy was beautiful,' he said.

'Mmm.' She shook her head. 'You remember when I said Noah was resourceful?

Austin nodded.

'Well, what I hadn't counted on was him using that resourcefulness to get his hands on drugs.'

Austin leaned forward but said nothing.

Lilly sighed. She put her two middle fingers around the sides of her headscarf and jiggled them backwards and forwards to adjust the fabric. 'I don't want to think of him as a victim, you know?

'Yea,' murmured Austin, 'but if he's not a victim, then what is he?'

Lilly wiped her eyes and then turned and sauntered after her husband, calling Aashirbaad's name as she went.

Austin dashed through the front door and straight down Leytonstone Road jumping into every puddle he came across. Halfway to the tube station, he stopped and leaned across the railings of an old graveyard. He could feel the frog doing leaps around his stomach again. *Fuck that.* He pulled out his iPhone to check the maps. Just then he got a pop-up notification of a new email.

Dear Austin,

I followed-up on that patient you mentioned meeting whilst in the A&E department. I am very sorry to tell you she died in hospital on that very same evening from complications related to her cancer. I have attached a newspaper clipping of the obituary. You might like to know that the attending physician, whom I have worked with his entire career, assured me she went peacefully.

I do hope you are keeping well. It was, may I say, a pleasure meeting a young person with such potential.

All the best,
Dr Tandy Newman

P.S.: The physician did say one other quite interesting thing. Apparently, Miss Jackson repeated the phrase 'Tell him thank you' several times before she lost consciousness. I would like to think she was referring to your kindness.

Austin took a deep breath in and hopped through another puddle. As the muddy water splashed onto his silk-blend chinos, he smiled. Perhaps the biggest smile he'd allowed himself in a long time.

At home later that afternoon, Austin set about rummaging through a box. This was an ordinary-looking box of the variety you might find stuffed with wintry attire or baby clothes grown too small. But this box, which began life as a catch-all repository, now held all the mistakes and secrets of Austin's life in physical form. There he placed ticket stubs and menu cards from old dates with boys he no longer knew, his report card from A levels where he failed maths, a love letter to his mother from the father he had never known, the HIV test results. Against his expectations, Austin did not get sentimental as he sorted through these things. They were shameful mementos, things that became a part of him but which he compartmentalised. Placed underneath a birthday card from his mother, he found the notebook from Florence. Reading it now it struck him how little of Noah was in those handwritten pages. He had opened the notebook hoping to find some solace, a happy memory from an otherwise fateful trip or perhaps some clue missed the first time round. But all he found were traces of himself, a self he no longer wanted to be.

A tricky silence of the mind followed. What had he expected to feel? For someone typically full of answers, it came us a sudden relief to Austin to just be still.

After some moments of sitting motionless, his mind filled with so many thoughts that he willed it to go blank. He put on his jacket and took the lift downstairs. In the entryway he ran into the security guard who doubled as building postman, a person who in better days would have been called a doorman. They exchanged a nod of the head and when recognition hit the guard, he called after Austin.

'You're the fella in flat 83?'

Austin turned around, expected to be handed a package.

'Your gentleman friend came round a couple days ago. He didn't have his key with him. He asked if you were in. I rang up, but I suppose you weren't home.'

It couldn't have been Noah, could it? 'Gentleman friend?' asked Austin.

'Yea, you'll pardon me for saying it, but the Muslim one.' He said this as if there were many men calling on the resident of flat 83, which couldn't have been further from the truth.

Austin leaned against the ledge of the sliding window separating the guard's enclave from the rest of the foyer. He wanted to know more. When precisely did this happen? Was it before Austin had gone to Noah's place? Why hadn't Noah mentioned it? What had Noah been wearing? Did he look distraught? But before he could ask a single one of these questions, a woman approached the window asking for her dry cleaning. Austin sighed and walked out the front door.

It was a perfect summery afternoon in Northwest London, almost too perfect. The rain cleared and the thermometer raised to twenty-five degrees, which was what locals called a heat wave. Because of this absurdly nice weather, Austin took off his jacket and tied it around his shoulders. He'd seen boys in The Hamptons do this once on a trip there in his twenties and had mimicked the move ever since. He walked past the cricket ground, the city council building, and carried on to Marylebone. When he came to Marble Arch, he crossed Hyde Park and sat on a stone bulwark at Speakers' Corner. He didn't expect much, only to be distracted from the nothingness that washed over him on the forty-minute walk. A man with greying hair and far too many wrinkles stood in a rather dapper suit holding a ceramic black Thermos. Propped next to him was a sign post which read *Blair would have made Protestant Religious Protest a criminal offence. The Labour party are against Freedom of religious expression.* This was the sort-of thing that could rev-up and revile Austin in equal accord, but now he couldn't have cared less. He untied his jacket and slipped it on again, turning towards Oxford Street.

Only last year, London teased him as a sterile kind of place. It was the place where he worked, ate, slept, got into trouble, and looked for ways of escape. Now it felt like an escape in itself. How odd that the very place embodying all your fears becomes the place precipitating all your hopes. Weaving in and out of pedestrian traffic on London's biggest shopping street was akin to the seventh layer of hell. Regent Street was only marginally better. It's amazing what the combination of grief, separation, and anger can do to a person. A two-mile walk through busy thoroughfares becomes a challenge; what would usually irritate you seems to have no effect; and the littlest of infractions — someone bumping into your shoulder or stepping on your hand-blasted loafers — is a hanging offence. He stopped to examine himself in the window of a vintage shop. He was altered, looking worse for the wear but somehow more put together on the inside. If internal beauty shines out, Austin had it in bounds.

When he reached Leicester Square, he let his feet do the thinking as they carried him into the boundless lobby of The National Gallery. By instinct, he took the staircase to the second level and then walked past the Central Hall through the great works of Northern Italian portraiture and into the Sainsbury Wing. He stopped in front of a massive painting of egg tempera on wood. The Dead Christ and Virgin, 1330s-40s, Giotto.

Austin's posture lengthened considerably and for a moment he felt as though the crown of his head might scrape the vaulted ceiling. Nearby, a tour guide masked as a would-be art critic stood discussing the painting with a small group of housewife-looking women. One of them asked about the application of paint and the smooth matte finish. The tour guide was explaining how tempera dries rapidly and is applied in thin, semi-opaque or transparent layers allowing for great precision. Another one of the women couldn't keep up and walked away to stare at a different canvas. Behind the tour guide, a small boy crouched out from behind the corpus of disinterested tourists. He wore an ankle-length, white robe, almost like a tailored t-shirt. Austin recognised it as a thobe. He'd seen pictures of Noah in one. At once, an incredible lightness slid into his body, a bizarre happiness coming from everywhere and nowhere. So much had happened in the preceding months, and yet it all paled in comparison to that wonderful little boy looking at a piece of art which had helped thrust Europe into the Renaissance. It felt, in a way, like Austin's own rebirth and he understood that every birth required a life-giving force. This almost pathological need to stand guard between his inner feelings and his mother, where had it come from?

How he failed to notice and appreciate all the things his own mother did for him. On a basic level he knew she made his childhood house safe and his life run smoothly, but how naive he had been to discount everything she'd done for him as an adult. He began to recognise all she contributed, not least of which was a listening ear — one with hard-wearing opinions, sure, but weren't his own strong opinions something he cherished? How rarely had he said 'thank you' that there was always someone on the other end of the line, that she remembered his birthday every year, that she baked his favourite pie, that she accepted him for who he was and what he had become? Though he wanted to demonise her for the all the inappropriate things she said and all the harm he imagined she caused with his father, he noticed there was a lot left undone if you took Millicent out of the picture. He should have been much more grateful and have told her so more often. She tried. She really did. Now she did have some issues of her own, but had he been paying more attention to her and to their relationship, rather than all the things that seemed more important at the time, both of them might have some shelter in each other, not just as mother and child, but as coadults. And what's left? When you strip away all the hurt of the boys that have wounded you and the work that always seems too much and the disease which will never heal, what's left? Only the people that matter. Only the ones loving you. Despite their problems, and regardless of yours.

We believe we can change the things around us that do not conform with how we think we ought to be seeing the world. There are so many 'if onlys' and 'what ifs' tied up in this way of thinking that it's no wonder things rarely work out in the way we anticipate. We do not think of the outcome of our actions on other people. We do not readily accept the consequences for our part in shaping how and what we become. And yet, when we do, when someone is brave enough to say, 'I played a part in this,' their desires suddenly and completely change. We are all in the pits of life, sooner or later, but those with real guts look up and out of the abyss. Austin allowed himself to feel now, a small concession; he alone owned the power to make his life better. Maybe radical change was not in the books for him, but small, everyday changes were — the kind of changes that allow oneself to wake everyday with the intent to live moment by moment, day by day with a renewed sense of what it means to be alive, knowing life is such a precious thing.

Heaven lies beneath the feet of mothers. Something Noah used to say. The phrase came back to Austin with such mental force it compelled him to pick up his iPhone and ring Milli, right there from Room 51 of The National Gallery. As though Noah himself were guiding Austin's fingers along the keyboard from beyond the grave, he nimbly punched each of the eleven digits. As the phone rang, his heart pounded like a wild animal trying to escape from his chest.

She picked up after two rings. 'Austin!'

Her excited tone caught him off guard, his hands so full of sweat that the phone case stuck to his palm. 'Uhh, hello mum.'

'I'm so glad to hear from you!'

What? Really? He felt, for the first time in his life, guilty for not keeping in better touch with her. 'I know you probably didn't expect to get this call, and I'm not sure how to start —'

'It's fine, Austin, really.' How she'd waited for this day!

'Please. Just let me finish, mum.' He worked up a whole speech in his mind by this point and no amount of unexpected enthusiasm on his mother's part would derail him. 'I'm sorry how we've acted toward each other these past few months and I just want to get back on good terms, or as best of terms as we can. We don't always see eye to eye, but I need you in my life. You're my mum and that's what matters.'

The phone line went quiet for several seconds.

'Uhm, hello, mum. Are you there?'

Her sobbing grew louder. 'I'm here, son, oh I'm here.'

That night, Austin slept soundly.

Acknowledgements

To my first readers: Jennifer Prince, Lali Sindi, Daniel Burger, Jeremy Shulman, and Charlotte Van de Sande.

Thanks furthermore,
- Jen, for your advice and constant faith in me.
- Lali, for the diligent copy editing.
- Daniel, for being a sounding board.
- J.S. and Gabriela Hirlea, for sharing your memories and dreams with me.
- Lisa Reardon, my writing coach at Gotham Writers Workshop where the initial concepts for this novel were born.

Early in the writing process, I was grateful to have some much-needed words of encouragement from Emma Woolf. Whenever I feel down or need some inspiration, I go back to those words, printed and pasted inside the cover of my journal. Thank you, Emma, for always knowing exactly what to say.

Exploring motherhood as a theme in this book unexpectedly helped me come to terms with my feelings for my mum and for all the women that have played a mothering role in my life at one point or another. To that end, I wish to thank those ladies, scattered all across this world and beyond, for their love and support.

And finally to my love Lester, whom I married just weeks after the draft was finished. Thank you for being my very first reader, typo-checker, and deadline enforcer.

Attribution Notes

The line 'There is such a shelter in each other' is from Pedigree by Nick Laird in *To a Fault*, published by Faber and republished in The Guardian.

Giotto's Pentecost (1310-8) is held in the National Gallery London, as is The Dead Christ and Virgin (c 1330s-40s) which is attributed to a Neapolitan follower of Giotto.

The line beginning 'Our whisper woke no clocks' is from WH Auden's poem The Dream.

The eulogy Lilly Hakim quotes is by Henry Scott Holland from his 1910 sermon titled *Death the King of Terrors*.

ABOUT THE AUTHOR

Jeremy C Bradley-Silverio Donato is the author of *Virginia Woolf and the Judicial Imagination*, a monograph based on his doctoral research. This is his first novel.

Follow him online @jeremycbradley